ON THE EDGE OF THE FJORD

Also By Alta Halverson Seymour

Timothy Keeps a Secret
Galewood Crossing
The Tangled Skein
A Grandma for Christmas
At Snug Harbor Inn
The Secret of the Hidden Room
The Christmas Stove: A Story of Switzerland
Arne and the Christmas Star (Norway)
The Christmas Donkey (France)
Kaatje and the Christmas Compass (Holland)
The Top o' Christmas Morning: A Story of Ireland
Erik and the Christmas Camera (Sweden)
When the Dikes Broke
Toward Morning: A Story of the
Hungarian Freedom Fighters
Charles Steinmetz

On the
Edge of the Fjord

By Alta Halverson Seymour

Illustrated by Harold Minton

BETHLEHEM BOOKS • IGNATIUS PRESS

Bathgate   San Francisco

Originally published by The Westminster Press, 1944

Cover art by Margaret Rasmussen, adapted from original
by Harold Minton
Interior artwork by Harold Minton
Chapter decorations by Margaret Rasmussen
Cover design by Theodore Schluenderfritz

All Rights Reserved

First Bethlehem Books Printing December 2015

ISBN 978-1-932350-46-3
Library of Congress Catalog Number: 2013957543

Bethlehem Books • Ignatius Press
10194 Garfield Street South
Bathgate, ND 58216
www.bethlehembooks.com
1-800-757-6831

Printed in the United States on acid-free paper

Manufactured by Thomson-Shore, Dexter, MI (USA); RMA101JM5409, February, 2016

To My Husband
my good companion up the fiords
and over the fields of Norway

Contents

 I

THE NAZIS COME TO VALCOS

"GOOD-BY, MARTIN! Good-by, my little Petra!" said Captain Engeland, and for a moment his eyes were troubled. He gave his son's hand a quick, firm shake. Then he gently rumpled his daughter's light curls and smiled down at her. "Petra was a funny name to give a dainty little thing like you," he chuckled. "It means rock, and somehow it doesn't quite fit you, but your mother wanted you named for your grandfather, Peter, and you know what a terror your mother is—she just will have her own way."

He winked at Petra, and she winked back, for they knew that in all of Norway it would be hard to find a gentler, sweeter-natured woman than Fru Engeland. Petra understood very well that her father was joking to keep his spirits up, and theirs too. She knew that he was reluctant to leave them for this trip up the coast to the fishing islands, for Martin was away at school all week, and she and her mother were alone with the two old servants in the big house on the edge of the fjord. She knew too that, as part owner and manager of the big fishing co-operative, he was obliged to go. He had

1

had to take these trips before, of course, but of late, to Petra's great delight, he had managed to conduct as much as possible of his business from his study at home or from his office in the big warehouse down at the foot of the fjord.

Fru Engeland, as well as Petra, knew all these things, and she knew something her fourteen-year-old daughter did not quite comprehend—the growing tension in the country, the uneasiness that no one liked to put into words. But she said gaily, as she patted her husband's cheek affectionately when he came to give her a good-by kiss: "Bring me a whale this time, Johann. You know you've always promised me one, but I haven't seen it yet."

"Take care of them, Martin," said the captain. "They're quite a pair. They may need watching."

"I'll do my best, sir," replied Martin, "but that's a big order." And all of them were smiling and waving as the boat moved down the fjord.

But as Fru Engeland and Petra sat talking with Martin on his week-end visit home a few weeks later, they were not smiling. Strange and terrifying news had come, news of Nazi troops in Oslo, in Bergen.

"And even here, in our little village, they will come," said Martin. "Even now, in our school, the Nazis are trying to change our history courses, telling our teachers what they shall teach us."

"And your teachers, are they obeying what the Nazis tell them?" asked Petra.

"What do you think?" returned Martin, rising and moving restlessly about the room. "Of course they are not. They are teaching Norwegian history as it really is—and you know it is a stirring history. Norsemen have always been brave and daring."

Petra nodded, but she had never cared so much as her brother did for history. She was far more interested in the present—in the party to be given at Signe's, for instance, or the hike up the mountain, or the summer festival. But now the present looked more forbidding than the past.

"What are we to do when the troops come?" she asked in a small voice. "They will not hurt us, will they?"

"They will expect you to give them anything they want that we have. Perhaps they will expect to quarter some officers here—it is a good, comfortable house."

"We cannot refuse that, of course," said Fru Engeland, but her voice was deeply troubled as she asked, "Martin, what of your father? They will know about his big boat, and the many smaller fishing vessels he controls. They must know how influential he is with the people." She paused and finished in a half whisper: "They may want to get hold of him and the boats. Have you thought of that?"

"I've not thought of much else," returned the boy. "I had hoped against hope that he might be here now, or that he could get home and away again before they come here."

"Perhaps we could reach him by telephone at the islands," ventured Petra.

"I tried that," admitted Martin, "but he had already left, intending, on his way home, to touch at one or two places where there are no phones."

"He will hear the radio," said Petra hopefully.

"But that is both conflicting and misleading," returned her brother.

"And the enemy wants boats," said their mother, putting into words the fear they all had. "They may want your father to give them special help—they may take him prisoner when he refuses."

"Of one thing I am sure—they won't get the boats from him. We need them ourselves to get men to England, where they can be outfitted and trained to fight. Yet, if the Nazis come here to Valcos, their big reason for coming will be to get hold of the boats," said Martin.

Petra looked at her mother's anxious face and said quickly, "But Father is too smart to walk right into a trap."

"Yes, but what if he doesn't know that the Nazis are here? What if he doesn't know the trap is set and waiting for him?" demanded her brother. "We have to look this squarely in the face, Petra. If the troops get here before Father does, we must find some way of warning him not to come home. You must manage somehow to come as fast as you can to the school and let me know."

"O Martin," said Petra fervently, as she said good-by to her brother the next morning. "I hope you will be here when they come."

Her brother replied as earnestly, "And so do I."

Certainly nobody in Valcos had expected the Nazis to arrive so soon. People were going quietly about their affairs that early evening, tending to the milking, the chickens, the fishing nets; the children playing in the village streets; the women preparing the evening meal, when someone on the pier cried out, "Here they come!"

Swiftly the news spread, and from houses, barns, and gardens came pale-faced people, watching the ships come nearer and nearer up the fjord. But as the enemy troops began setting foot on the pier, people turned, with stony faces, into their houses and shut the doors. It was as if they could not bear to see hostile forces in streets that had been peaceful for centuries, as if they could shut out the intruders by going into their homes and barring the doors.

Petra, crouching in the inglenook, heard marching feet coming up the street, heard orders barked, knew that men were stopping, in small detachments, at the houses of the neighbors. She wondered what she would do when that dreadful knock came at their own door, for her mother was down at the other end of the village caring for a sick neighbor. And though old Helga and Anna were at home, they would be too frightened to be of much help. She would have to face the soldiers, answer their questions, listen to their orders. Oh, if only Martin were here!

They were at the next house. She could see them going up the steps. Now, a sharp order out in front, steps across the porch, three, heavy knocks at the door! Petra put her hands on the chair arms and tried to rise, but she could not force herself into action.

"Open at once, or we batter in the door," the harsh order was shouted.

Petra, knowing well that they meant exactly what they said, straightened her shoulders, lifted her chin, and managed to walk to the door, unlock it, and pull it open.

A group of Nazi officers stood there, a stern-faced captain in command. He looked a little surprised as he saw the slender, fair-haired girl, but his eyes grew hard again as he snapped: "Your father, miss. He need not try to hide behind you. You speak German?"

Petra bowed assent, but her eyes were blazing. As if her proud and brave father would try to hide behind anyone! "My father is not at home," she jerked out.

"Your mother, then!" demanded the captain.

"She also is away from home," said Petra, between stiff lips.

"They have not taught you very good manners. Have you not learned to invite guests to enter the house?"

"Guests!" exclaimed Petra, and now her head was high. "I see no guests."

"You'll see plenty of them," sneered the officer, "and the more polite you are, the better it will be for you and your family." He turned to the others. "Come in, gentlemen, we are graciously invited to take supper here. Tell the servants, young lady, that some officers are here to supper, and come back at once to see to the entertainment of your guests."

Petra was only too glad of an excuse to get away. In the kitchen she found Anna and Helga terrified. It took a great deal of cajoling to make them stop huddling together in a corner and start supper preparations

for the uninvited guests. When Petra left the kitchen, she went for a moment into the back garden, straining her eyes in the hope of seeing her mother hurrying along the back road.

"But no, she cannot leave Fru Ostrander until someone comes to relieve her," she thought. "Mother knows that I am close to neighbors and Anna and Helga are here. I must stop this trembling. Norwegians are brave, Father and Martin always say, and I am a Norwegian. I must not disgrace them, and I'm not going to, either!"

One impossible plan after another flashed through her mind as she stood there—heroic plans for saving her father, Valcos, Norway. Then a harsh voice cut into her flying thoughts, "You are wanted in the living room, miss."

"You were gone long enough," growled the captain when she entered. "Now tell us, Where is your father? When will he return?"

"I do not know," replied Petra promptly.

A skeptical grunt, and: "We will come back to that later. Where is your mother?"

"Caring for a sick neighbor on the other side of the village."

"That may be true enough. Now, your father owns a large share in the fisheries, and has his own ship. Don't deny it. We know well enough. We know he controls many boats. When is he expected home?"

The question was barked at her with a suddenness that made her jump, but she managed to reply stiffly, "I do not know."

"Well, we have ways of finding out without your help, if you're going to be obstinate. But we can be more lenient with you and your family if you will co-operate a little. We can get your father's boat easily enough, and the others too. It is not so much of a boat," he added, looking at the girl with cool sarcasm, "but we can use it and the others too. We need shipping space for the things your country-men will so kindly consent to give us to aid us in the war."

Petra's eyes were blazing and her lips were trembling in her effort to keep from sending a fiery answer back to this insolent young officer. But she had suddenly realized that he was trying to goad her into a retort that would give him the information he wanted, and in her need a plan of action sprang into her mind.

"Since my father and mother are not here," she forced herself to say politely, "may I inquire what you need here besides your supper, which will soon be ready?"

"Ah, that is a better tone," said the officer, some-what mollified. "We require sleeping quarters as well. Four of us will be your permanent guests."

That would complicate matters, for Petra knew she must manage to get out of the house tonight, unseen by anyone. Well, they could have the guest room, and she would give up her own lovely room. That would provide a good excuse to get the things together that she needed, as well as a little necessary time for her preparations.

"We will prepare the rooms while you eat your supper," she said, still politely, "and here is Anna to say that it is served."

"We would like your company," said the officer, polite in his turn.

"I must see to the preparation of your rooms," replied Petra, wondering how long she could manage to avoid sitting down with these unwelcome guests.

Up to her room she flew, and straight to her desk. From a small drawer she took a compass, a tiny flashlight, and a queer little whistle. These she stuffed into the pocket of a heavy sweater. Next came a pair of blue slacks, a scarf, and a dark knitted square to tie around her head. Heavy gloves, socks, and boots were added, and all were made into a neat roll and placed in a corner of her mother's closet. Then she began the real dismantling of the room. It was hard to think of those arrogant officers quartering themselves here with careless ease. But she was too intent on thinking out the details of her plan to grieve.

Mother was not coming, it seemed. Could it be that the Nazis were not allowing anyone to leave the houses tonight? That would be awkward, indeed, for the success of her plan, but she would manage somehow.

She hoped that she would be allowed to telephone her mother to assure her of her safety. If only she could telephone Father! One thing was certain, he and his boat must not fall into the hands of these arrogant Nazis!

Tonight, after everyone was asleep, she would slip out in her warm, dark clothing, and with the aid of her compass and small flashlight, would get to Martin by the mountain trail through the woods. It was a difficult trail she knew that well enough—and harder still by night. But she would manage it. Near the school, she would use the whistle to give a signal her brother knew well. Together they would get word to Father somehow.

The officers were still at table when Fru Engeland, her face pale, her eyes full of apprehension, came hurrying through the back garden and into the kitchen. Petra saw her coming, and, thankful that she herself had worked so fast, was ready.

"It's strange," she thought, as she ran down the back stairs, "I feel years older than I did an hour ago. No use telling myself I'm not frightened, but at least I can tell Mother things are pretty well in hand."

By the kitchen door, they clung together for a moment; then Petra softly told of the arrangements she had made for the officers. "I'm trying to be polite to them," she whispered. "It seems to be the best way. I gave up my room. I'll move in with you."

"Petra," her mother whispered in return, "there was a letter from Father in the post office when I stopped on my way over to Ostranders'. He docks soon—perhaps even tomorrow."

Petra nodded, but her heart went down into her shoes. All her careful planning was of no use now! There would be no time to get over the mountain to Martin. She would have to get the word to Father herself.

But now the officers, back in the living room, had asked for their hostess. Petra watched proudly as her

mother answered their questions with a vague politeness that baffled them. Mother, the quickest of them
all at games that required a ready wit, was pretending
not to be very bright. Petra wanted to rush over and
hug her.

It seemed to her that the house would never settle
down. The officers were in no mood to retire early, and
when at last they were quiet, Fru Engeland was wide
awake, talking in whispers. Even when her mother
slept at last, Petra lay quietly trying to work out details
of her new plan. Her first scheme had been terrifying enough, but the new one was far more difficult
and dangerous.

It was toward morning when she slipped quietly
out of bed, put on her slippers and dark robe, scooped
up her handle, her heart pounding fast as she tiptoed
down the back stairs and into the kitchen. There she
swiftly donned her dark clothing, hid her slippers and
robe, packed up some rye bread and cheese, and went
out into the early morning, thankful, for once, that a
fog hung over the valley. For though it did slow her
progress, it gave her a little protection, and surely, she
knew, she needed it.

Familiar though she was with the terrain, it was
hard to find her way. But she got down to the cove at
last where her little sailboat was docked, the boat her
father had taught her to sail when she was ten. "Every
Norwegian girl should know how to sail a boat and do
it well," he had said.

"Especially if she is the daughter of Norway's best
sailor," she had replied gaily.

There was almost no wind this morning, and Petra slipped the oars into place, thankful that she knew how to feather them so that they made almost no sound. If only she could get safely away from Valcos, where the Nazis might be on a special watch for her, she believed she would be able to get all the way down the fjord where many boats fished in the quiet waters. But she was fishing, she thought grimly, for a bigger take than any of them.

Through the fog came the muffled sound of a boat. Was it a patrol boat? No one else would be out in this fog, surely. What if they should touch? What if the fog should lift a little and they should catch sight of her? She stopped rowing and held her breath. But the boat slipped by her in the fog.

She knew well enough how rocky this coast was, and felt thankful for her compass, and that her father had taught her how to use it. Now the fog was beginning to clear and a little breeze was springing up at last. That would help, and she set her sail. Her tired arms told her that she had rowed to good purpose, and as the fog lifted she saw that she had left the village some distance behind her. Now the wind was springing up merrily, and she got her fishing equipment from the box where she kept it, safe and dry, under the seat. It would be in plain sight if anyone challenged her, and sometime during the morning she would really use it.

Here came a boat now, straight toward her. She felt sick and faint when she saw that it was indeed manned by the enemy. But she managed to answer so simply, though her teeth were chattering, that she was allowed to go on.

She knew well enough what she must do. And she knew, too, that every moment counted. She must get down the fjord to where it joined the sea, to the warehouses where she would find her father's good friend and partner, Herr Jorgenson. He might be able to get in touch with Father by radio. At least he could surely send a fast boat with a message.

She was heartily glad now for the hours she had spent on the fjord. Every cove, every little fishing bay was familiar to her, and now that the fog had lifted she kept a careful lookout for patrol boats, slipping into a sheltered cove or throwing out her fishline if she saw one approaching.

She came now to where the fjord widened, the shore line smoothed out. Here there was no protection, no hiding place, and there were certain to be patrols. Sure enough, one came toward her almost at once.

"I can't let them turn me back," she thought, "so near my goal."

She greeted the crew politely and waved as she went by. One of the hardest things to manage was the politeness which she was forcing herself to use toward these intruders. But, just as at home, it paid dividends, for the boatmen seemed to feel she was friendly toward them. They waved in turn and called a greeting.

Now she was almost at Herr Jorgenson's. But here came another boat, straight up to her, and a volley of harsh questions was fired at her. Her heart was pounding, but, remembering her mother's technique of the night before, she pointed to her lunch and her fishing equipment, shaking her head with such a vague and bewildered smile at their questions that one of the officers said impatiently: "She knows nothing! An ignorant fishing girl!" To her great relief, the boat chugged away without giving her further trouble.

Now if she could just get around the bend to the little quay in front of Herr Jorgenson's office and packing house! Other boats lay at anchor there, and she would have a good chance of tying up without being noticed. She didn't dare to try to make too much speed, and those last minutes, breathless though they were, seemed longest of all. At last she drew near the other boats. She had arrived!

Making her boat fast, she climbed up on the pier, and almost flew up the stairs to the office. There, first to her surprise and delight, then to her alarm, stood her father.

"O Father!" she cried. "You shouldn't be here! I came to warn you. You must go away as fast as you can!"

"What a welcome!" said her father smiling, though he was as surprised to see her as she was to see him. "Now, my little Petra, why did you come?"

Together the men listened to the story which Petra quickly told them. And when the short recital was finished, she saw that her father's eyes were shining and that he nodded when Herr Jorgenson cleared his throat and said: "We needn't worry about Norway. With youngsters like this, we'll come through."

"They want your boat, Father, and the fishing boats. And they mustn't have them. We are going to need them, Martin says, to get men out of here to England."

"Yes, little daughter. I suspected trouble and left my big boat at the islands. I came in on a small fishing boat, and we'll go home together."

"O Father, that would be lovely," said Petra wistfully, "but it is just simply impossible. That's why I came to warn you. You mustn't come home." And she told of the officers who had moved in upon them, of the questions they had asked, of the use they meant to make of her father's boat and of the fishing fleet.

"That puts a different light on it," said her father thoughtfully. "Petra, can you sail back up the fjord with instructions to Herr Ostrander of how to get the boats away, one at a time, as many as can be spared, leaving only enough for some fishing? Can you carry such instructions in your head, so as to have no telltale messages?"

"Of course I can," said Petra firmly, "if you'll just stay away, Father, for they would surely take you prisoner if you went home. They want those boats."

"And, between us, we will see that they don't get them," promised her father.

"And you, Father, what are you going to do?" asked Petra.

"That I can't tell you," answered her father, "because when the officers ask about me, I want you to be able to say you don't know where I am or what I am doing. And indeed I scarcely know myself where

I shall be, though I have a good idea of what I will try to do. But I can promise you I will be making myself useful and will get word home when I can." Putting both arms around his daughter, he held her close for a moment, then said proudly: "My Petra has lived up to her name. And now sit down, my daughter, and rest while we figure out the instructions for Ostrander."

There was a swift consultation, then Petra's father said: "Now we shall give you the instructions. Listen carefully. Are you sure you can remember something quite complicated?"

Petra nodded. "Oh, yes, I can, even though I shall look like this if I am stopped for questions." And she put on a dull and stupid air that made her father and Herr Jorgenson laugh in spite of their anxiety for her.

"You don't look as if you could do much harm to the Nazi cause," said her father, "though you'll be keeping plenty of boats away from them, and doing your part to get men away too."

In short, terse words Captain Engeland gave his daughter the plan of action and detailed instructions, ending with the reassurance: "I think this can all be done in such a natural way that the Nazis won't know what's happening until a good many of our men are on their way to England in these boats. Martin will be a big help with that too."

"Oh, yes! Martin will get home this week-end if he possibly can." There was relief and joy in Petra's face at the thought of her brother's home-coming, for Martin could handle this part of it, she knew, far better than she could. "And now I must get back or they will surely suspect I have been up to something."

"And take with you," said Herr Jorgenson, "a basket of fish. That may save you time and explanations."

The sun was high when Petra tied up at the home pier and ran to the house, her basket on her arm. In the home garden, the officers were having midmorning coffee.

"You have been away!" said the officer in charge, accosting her sharply. "You are not supposed to go without permission."

"Our supplies are not great," said Petra quietly. "I knew where to get fish for lunch. The best fishing is early. No one but myself was up."

Her mother, waiting anxiously in the kitchen, overheard this conversation. "Did you really go fishing?" she asked softly, when Petra came into the house.

"Here's the proof," said Petra, holding out her basket. In her relief at being home, she chuckled. "Come upstairs, Mother," she added in a low tone. "I'll tell you all about it. I never in all my life had a better fishing trip, but it wasn't exactly for the Nazis' lunch. It was for Father and Norway."

They had reached their room now, and as they closed the door, Fru Engeland put her hands on her daughter's shoulders and looked at her searchingly. "Petra," she said, "you have done something important this morning. I can see it in your eyes. You seem to have grown up overnight. Now tell me about it. We will work together."

Her eyes were solemn as Petra told her story, and at the anxiety in her face Petra said, smiling a little: "But what I did this morning was only the beginning, Mother. The hardest part is left. Now we've got to manage some way to get the boats off for England. Father sent word by me to Herr Ostrander."

"Ostrander?" echoed her mother, and there was doubt in her voice. "He would be the logical one, of course, but, Petra, I question whether he has the courage. I was there last night, you know, caring for his wife, when he came home, and I've seldom seen a more thoroughly frightened man. He is terrified of the Nazis. Not that I blame him!" She stopped short, her eyes deeply troubled.

"Of course Father didn't know that," said Petra, looking anxious.

"No. No one can tell how folks are going to react these days. I already see that people will surprise us. I would not have expected this of Herr Ostrander. His wife, ill though she was, was far more courageous." She paused and smiled down at Petra. "You, my gay little daughter—I would not have expected you to work out a plan like your fishing trip, or to be so brave."

"I wasn't so brave, Mother. I was as scared as could be. My teeth were chattering most of the way," said Petra, shaking her head. "But, O Mother," she burst out, "Herr Ostrander's just got to get himself together and show some courage. We must get those boats off, and fast, Father said. If only I could get away again! If only I could get to Martin!"

II

MARTIN AND PETRA GO FISHING

"PETRA!"

The call was insistent, but very low, and Petra, down on her knees in the kitchen garden, did not pause in her work, though her heart beat fast as she answered softly, "Listening!" Certainly that sounded like her brother Martin.

It was almost a week now since the Nazi troops had come to the little village of Valcos, almost a week since she had taken her sailboat down the fjord to warn her father not to come home. Daily she had been hoping to find out that Herr Ostrander had got some of the boats off for England, but each day she had been disappointed. If only Martin could get home this week end, together they could surely do something about those boats!

Petra had learned a great deal in that week of Nazi occupation. For one thing, she had learned to be very quiet, for a Nazi soldier seemed always within hearing, and Otto, the stout, red-faced orderly who had taken Martin's room a day or two ago, was constantly turning up in unexpected places. But Petra exulted to herself

20

as she thought triumphantly that not a single Nazi had learned of her trip down the fjord to her father, nor of the message she carried back to Herr Ostrander.

"We must work fast," her father had said. "Some of those boats must get off without delay."

But Herr Ostrander was not working fast. The Nazis were watching very closely, he said, and she knew well enough that that was true. But she knew too that if some of those boats did not get off soon, it would be too late. She longed for the week end, and Martin's visit. And yet—over and over the question had whirled in her mind—would Martin be allowed to come? Controls were being tightened, she had known all too well. But, much as she had longed for Martin, she had feared too, lest his fiery tongue and his stubbornness get him into trouble. But surely he would control himself. For he would know well that there was important work to be done. He would know that helpers were desperately needed. Yes, Martin would find some way to come, she felt sure, if it were in any way possible.

When he did come, she meant to talk to him before the officers did. There were things he would need to know. So she had stationed herself in the kitchen garden, knowing that no one could question her right to be there, and sure that Martin would find her, for the back garden lay in full view of the path down which he would come.

Now the long-awaited call had come: "Petra!"

It was Martin all right, and a great surge, half of joy, half of fear, swept over her. How much did he know? How much would she have an opportunity to tell him? At least he knew that the soldiers were there, for he had taken care to reconnoiter before he made his appearance. Martin, like herself, was learning caution.

"Shall I do any harm to you or Mother if I show myself?" he asked now, in a low voice.

"Come along," she answered softly. "Just kneel down here and help me with this weeding. The garden's about the only place we can talk."

She knew well enough where her brother was. Under the tall hedge at the end of the garden was a fine hiding place where the two of them had often taken refuge in days when all the village children were playing "hide-and-seek." Now she realized that it had come into service once more. In a moment her brother had slipped out and was kneeling beside her, his hands as busy as hers, as she told him, in swift, short sentences, the events of the week.

"You mean to say you sailed down the fjord all by yourself, swarming as it was with patrol boats, and found Father and warned him not to come home and brought the message back to Herr Ostrander?" Martin's tone was so full of surprised respect that Petra flushed with pleasure and gave an embarrassed little nod. "Girl, you've always said you didn't care much for history," he said, "but you surely helped to make it that time."

"It was just something that had to be done, Martin," murmured his sister, but she gave a pleased smile at a handful of weeds she had just pulled, for her brother's rare praise sounded very sweet to her. "The

Nazi patrols thought I was a fisher girl, and let me through, and indeed I did do a little fishing. I do some every day, as a matter of fact. It gives me a little freedom, and, besides, we need the fish."

"You certainly did a good job of fishing that day," replied Martin, laughing. "Now, Petra, how much progress has been made in getting the boats off to England?"

"None at all! Herr Ostrander says we have to proceed with great caution, that the boats are not by any means fitted for so long a journey, and it takes time to assemble the men who wish to go."

Martin frowned. "Ostrander is too cautious," he said. "Father has always seen to it that the company boats were kept in excellent condition. And as for the men and boys who want to go to England to join the forces, they would swamp our fishing fleet overnight if it were known that boats were available. I don't like the sound of this, Petra. Sounds as if the Nazis had frightened Herr Ostrander out of his good sense."

"They've frightened more than Herr Ostrander, Martin," said Petra, jabbing viciously at a weed. "You haven't seen them in action around here. Here's something to remember, Martin. Don't let them know you understand German very well. They're not much good at Norwegian, and it will hinder them in questioning you. I've been able to get on with them because I force myself to be polite to them. I can accomplish more that way. It's terribly hard, but I hope you will try to do the same."

"That's all right for a girl," Martin was beginning, when a warning nudge from his, sister stopped him.

He himself had heard nothing, but Petra's week of careful listening had sharpened her ears, and an instant later Otto, the orderly, stood before them.

"You are wanted in the house at once, boy," he said brusquely. "You should have reported to the captain the moment you arrived."

Martin jumped to his feet, his head thrown back. "This is my home," he said defiantly, in fair enough German. "When my father is away, I am master here."

The guard looked at him contemptuously. "I advise you not to take that tone with Captain Ebert," he said, jerking his head toward the house. "Go on, now. Be quick!"

Petra sprang up, shook as much garden dirt as possible from her hands, and started down the path after her brother.

"Your presence is not required, miss," said the soldier sharply. But quick-witted Petra took refuge, as she had often done that week, in a vague lack of understanding. "Thank you, yes," she replied, with a polite effort at German. "I will go at once, thank you. The captain wishes to see us."

"Where is your father?" was the question that was barked at Martin as he entered the study where the captain sat at the big desk with his back to the room.

"I don't know, sir," replied Martin, and indeed that was strictly true, for Captain Engeland had kept his whereabouts a secret from his family so far.

"You know well enough, and you had better tell us. Also his big boat. We want that."

"I don't know where they are, sir," Martin answered, and Petra was relieved to see that he had taken her hint and was speaking politely.

Captain Ebert swung swiftly around now and looked the boy over, from head to foot. "We need your father's help, and we propose to get it," he said, speaking with a deliberate emphasis that made Martin clench his fists in his effort to keep his temper. "And we will get his big boat. You may as well help us first as last. These little boats"—he nodded contemptuously toward the small harbor, where a part of the fishing fleet lay—"they will do to send small goods that we will need from your country. We will take them, of course, but they are far from being enough to transport all the supplies your neighbors and countrymen will so generously furnish us."

He smiled unpleasantly as he spoke, and Petra realized that he was trying to goad Martin into speech that would give away secrets, just as he had done to her at first.

Martin looked straight back at the captain, but he was conscious of his sister's tense position, her compressed lips, and once more he forced himself to say politely enough, in stumbling German, "I really can't help you, sir."

The captain bit his lip and frowned. The interview was not going to his satisfaction at all. As a matter of fact, he was finding the Engeland family annoyingly baffling. They saw to it that he could make no complaint of their hospitality: he and the members of his staff quartered there were well fed and well

cared for. Fru Engeland and Petra both seemed in-
telligent enough in some ways, yet all questions
were answered—politely enough, it was true—with
a certain vagueness that was far more irritating than
straight defiance would have been. He could have
dealt with defiance, readily enough. He had obviously
hoped for more satisfactory dealings with Martin. The
boy would fight back, he felt sure. He would collar
him the moment he came home and before he could
talk to the family. He would find out from him all he
needed to know, he'd see to that. And now, here came
the two together, and the boy was as bad as the others.

"Go now; we will come back to this later," he
said curtly.

"If you please," Petra said hesitatingly, "our supplies are dwindling sadly. There is not much for
supper. But the captain is fond of mountain trout.
With your permission, my brother and I will see if we
can find some in the lake a little way up the mountain."

"Very well," said the captain, who, as Petra well
knew, loved to eat. "Go then."

They were well on their way before Martin spoke,
for the interview and his strong effort at self-control
had unnerved him somewhat. Besides, they were
afraid of being overheard. But now he shook himself
as if he wanted to be rid of the whole thing. Then he
grinned down at his sister. "That was shrewd of you,
Petra. And you used to be such a gay, carefree little
monkey. You know, you are quite a surprise to me."

"I've had a week's training," she replied demurely,
"and haven't you always said that Norwegians were

brave and clever? We never could have got away for a walk together, but the captain is really worried about our supplies, and he has a weakness for mountain trout. We'd better get some, that's all."

"They're planning to use those boats soon, I'm sure of that," said Martin, changing swiftly to the subject in the thoughts of both. "That's probably—at least partly—why he made so light of them. Now, you said Father planned that they should go one or two at a time so as not to be too noticeable, and he said we ought to act fast. So far not one has gone. Tonight we get them started. I will see to that."

"O Martin!" cried Petra, drawing in her breath sharply. "Must you do it? Couldn't we talk again to Herr Ostrander?"

"What good would that do? You've already done that, more than once. But if we show him that a boy can do something, surely he would be ashamed not to follow suit."

"But how can you get things ready so soon? How will you get word around? That will be terribly danger-ous. The soldiers will be watching. I know."

"Petra," said Martin, shaking his head and smiling a little, "you almost had me worried. For a minute there you sounded like Ostrander. None of that now! You yourself weren't too afraid to do your part in the face of danger. Now you mustn't be afraid to let me do mine."

Petra swallowed hard and then nodded. "I know," she agreed. "But at least let me help, Martin."

"Yes, you have your part to do. You must catch the fish for the captain's supper, and meantime I will go a roundabout way down the mountain, and I will get word to the Ostergaard boys, and to the Holms and the Torgersons and a few more. Two boatloads should go, to help each other in case of need."

"O Martin, do be careful! You mustn't be seen and caught doing this!"

"I know. I'll take great care. I've been planning it out. I knew the time would come before long, and this is it. Tonight is the dark of the moon. And your good thought about the trout got us away from home. We might not be so fortunate again soon. We simply must not let this opportunity slip by."

"And if a soldier should spy upon me here and demand to know where you are, what shall I say?"

"From what I've seen and heard today, I think I can safely leave that to you."

"And you?" asked his sister, her heart beating painfully. "Are you going with the boats tonight?"

Martin looked down at her, his eyes so bright and eager she knew well what his answer would be. "Oh, yes, Petra! I've got to go. I want to get to England. Train for a flier! I hate to leave you and Mother," he added stumblingly, seeing the distress in her face, "but I've got to go where I'll be the most use. I have a feeling Father's there. Maybe we can work together. Maybe," he said, with an anxious glance at her, "we can come for you and Mother—or get you out in some way soon."

Petra nodded and gave him a motherly little pat on the shoulder. His anxious, questioning look showed his need of her help, and steadied her. "Well," she said briskly, "there's plenty to be done between now and suppertime. We'll meet again at the fork near the foot of the mountain. And then," she smiled up at him, "we will compare the results of our fishing."

Yes, she thought, as she walked on alone, no one could blame Martin for wanting to go with the other boys. It was dangerous business, but just about everything was dangerous these days. She longed to have him stay and yet felt she must not try to hold him back.

In spite of her anxiety about her brother, it was with a feeling of relief that she pushed the little boat out into the lake. For the first time in almost a week, she had a feeling of freedom. "They couldn't reach me here even if they wanted to," she thought grimly. "There's only one boat."

She had almost filled her basket when a shout made her turn so sharply that she rocked the boat. The stout Nazi guard stood on the shore, puffing from his climb. "Your brother—where is he?" he barked.

"Oh, my brother?" said Petra innocently. "Why, we came fishing, with the captain's permission."

"Yes, yes, I know. But your brother. Where is he?"

"Oh, fishing around somewhere," she replied vaguely, but she was thinking fast as she baited her hook. Had Otto overheard any of their conversation on the way up? No, she shook off that fear at once. They had been speaking in Norwegian, of which Otto understood very little. Anyway, she and Martin must have been fairly well on their way before he started, and the steeper parts of the trail, which she and her brother took as easily as mountain goats, would slow

Otto up as he puffed onward. She almost laughed as she pictured his climb. But she must get rid of him somehow, and without delay. He might be a trifle slow, but he was very thorough. He had been sent to check up on Martin, and it would not be easy to shake him off, she knew that. He might start hunting around on his own account; he might find Martin—the Holms' farm was not very far away. He might simply stay right here until she went home, sure that he would discover Martin in that way. It would never do for him to wait around until she went, and encounter Martin meeting her down the mountain.

She could think of only one thing to do, and she acted promptly. With a sharp movement, she managed to overturn the boat. "Help! Help!" she cried frantically. "Help!"

Otto looked at her in disgust, but he couldn't let her drown, for she was the one who helped to make the place comfortable for all of them, and even now Captain Ebert was looking forward to a delicious supper of her providing. "Hang onto that boat until I get my shoes off," he ordered, and plunged in. He was a clumsy swimmer, especially in his uniform, and Petra had hard work not to laugh as she watched his floundering efforts. But at last he reached her, and together they pushed the boat shoreward and righted it.

"Now look at me!" he sputtered, as he stood dripping on shore. "And the captain's supper. What of that?"

"I am so sorry," murmured Petra. "You must go home at once and get dry clothing. You would be no help whatever to the captain if you were ill. He would not like that. I have a dry coat here on shore. I will put that on, and I have more fishing tackle in the little locker in the boat. We will catch more fish. Hurry, now. We will soon be home. You tell Mother what happened, and she will see that you have a hot drink and are made comfortable."

Otto looked slightly bewildered at these quick, well-organized plans, but he was used to taking orders, and these sounded very sensible, especially that last sentence.

"Yes, yes," he answered. "I have found you. You are fishing. I have saved your life. I will go. You and your brother will soon be home. I have saved your life," he repeated with pride.

"I thank you," said Petra, wondering what Otto would think if he knew she had won last summer's swimming tournament in Valcos. "You'd better hurry now."

Even with her dry coat on, she was shivering as she rowed out again. Fortunately, the fishing was good, and she soon had enough trout for her purpose.

"Oh, I hope I won't keep Martin waiting," she thought, as she half slid, half scrambled down the mountain in her haste. What if they should find him standing there at the fork? What if they should send someone else to take Otto's place? But no, they could hardly do that. Otto was not fast, and the path was difficult. By the time he got home, it would be too late to send anyone else.

But Martin was not there when she reached the fork, and her anxiety grew as she waited. Had they discovered him as he went on his messenger's journey? Perhaps even now they were questioning him—and this would not be the routine questioning they had experienced before; it would be far more serious. Her heart beat fast. O Martin! Hurry! Hurry!

III

THE BOATS SAIL OUT

MARTIN WAS THINKING fast and clearly as he struck out on a little-used path he knew through the woods. Sigurd Holm was the one he wanted to see first. Together he and Sigurd would make plans. Sigurd would know more about the lay of the land than he did, for he had been here during all the days of the Nazi occupation. Martin had hunted and fished and sailed with him enough to know that the older boy had good judgment and great reliability. After the Holms, he would get word to the Ostergaards and the Torgersons and the Haugs. Perhaps Sigurd or one of the other Holm boys could help with that.

He remembered the warning the school's headmaster, Herr Professor Roland, had given him that morning—a warning that he should be cautious. He remembered his sister's more recent, "They may be watching you." If only he could in some way attract Sigurd's attention without making himself too prominent! Then he almost chuckled in sudden relief, for he had just remembered an old birdcall the

33

boys had often used in times past. Sigurd would be almost sure to be out in the fields today. He would use the old signal.

There were plenty of hiding places on the side of the mountain, and when Martin was forced to leave the protection of the wood, he took refuge in a pile of boulders that overlooked the Holm farm. Yes, Sigurd and Harald were both out, hard at work in the field. Martin gave his birdlike whistle, hoping the boys would remember it. No sign of recognition came. Again Martin whistled, and again, and at last he saw Sigurd hesitate in his work. He seemed to be saying something to his brother. Then he started across the field. Martin heard him call, "I'm going up to the spring for a drink." Soon he had disappeared into the wood, and Martin, choosing his way carefully, followed.

"Martin!" said Sigurd, without wasting a word. "Is it about the boats?"

"Yes," replied Martin swiftly. "How did you know?"

"Ostrander. He told me your father wanted some of the boats to go to England, and plenty of us are ready and anxious to go. Ten men to a boat. But Ostrander is afraid to give the word. I'm afraid the Nazis are getting to him, Martin. I d like to get him out of here. He's scared as a rabbit, and he knows your father's plans. He could do some harm without meaning to. He says the boats are not in condition to go, and he can't get them ready with the Nazis watching every move so closely."

"They're ready, Sigurd," said Martin proudly. "You know Father always saw to it that the boats were in the best of condition. Can you be ready to sail tonight?"

"Of course," answered Sigurd quietly, "we've just been waiting for this."

"Then see to it that Ostrander is on board. Ole Haug used to have the job managing the fleet here in the harbor. He can take it over again if necessary."

For the first time Sigurd smiled. "You can't scare Ole, even if he is well up in his seventies," he said. "And Herr Ostrander will be better off in England, if you can persuade him."

"We can persuade him," said Martin dryly. "Now, how do we get word to the others, Sigurd? I can go to the Torgersons, the Ostergaards, the—"

"Not the Torgersons," Sigurd interrupted, his blue eyes cold with anger. "You can't trust them, Martin. Every day Hans has come over to ask me if some of us aren't going to take the boats to England, but I never let on that I know a thing. He acts anxious to go, but, Martin," Sigurd stopped as if he could hardly bring out the words, "twice I've seen him walking with Lieutenant von Berg—talking and laughing. He didn't know I saw him. Hardly anyone here will speak to the Nazis, or even look at them. No, we daren't let Hans know one word of our plans. Quisling!"

The scorn and bitterness that went into that word told Martin more than many words could have done of the deep feeling that had stirred the little community in a few short days.

"Hans!" he cried. "I can't believe it! What, then, of Arne Ostergaard? I had thought you could take charge of one boat, and Arne of the other."

A look of delight chased the bitterness from Sigurd's face. "I in charge of one of the boats? Good! And you can trust Arne. No question of that."

The boys planned swiftly. Sigurd had means of getting word quickly to the boys who were ready to make up the first two boatloads. He and Harald and one or two others would take care of that. Martin would go to see Ole Haug.

"We'll get Ole to shift the *Rainbow* and the *Wave Rider* where we can load them easily tonight. No one will notice it for he sometimes sails the *Rider* and often works around the harbor. Also I must go to see Ostrander," said Martin. "Persuade him to go."

"How do you intend to do that, I should like to know?" asked Sigurd.

"Well, something will have to be done about the sentries. I suppose they must be tied up and left there until they are found in the morning. Herr Ostrander wouldn't like to be held responsible for that. Might get him into serious trouble. But if he is gone, who is to be blamed? No one is in charge."

"Martin, you have a head," said Sigurd, laughing. "You're coming with us, I hope."

"Try to keep me away," returned Martin. "And now for the ways and means, Sig."

All week Sigurd had been working and planning, and now as the boys discussed his plans and Martin's, they were found to dovetail well. Each boy had thought of some things that the other had not, and decisions were soon reached.

"Now, we're all set, I think," said Martin. "We meet between eleven and twelve in the cove above the harbor. It will be pretty dark, for it's the dark of the moon, and clouding up besides. Sure they can all find their way?"

"Trust them for that. And we're thankful to have the darkness for cover."

"Your father and Herr Dr. Ostergaard can take care of the sentries, you are sure?"

"Of course. But, Martin, who will watch your house? The officers are quartered there, you know, and that orderly, Otto. Someone should give the alarm if they are aroused."

"Petra will do that. We mustn't let any more people than absolutely necessary know our plans."

"Petra will be the one," agreed Sigurd with satisfaction, "you can bank on her."

Now Martin cut through the wood and came out above the Haug place. Ole himself was in the garden shed, and his faded blue eyes grew keen and alert as Martin talked.

"You can count on me, boy, and your plan is good. Only one thing—" he hesitated.

"What is that" asked Martin, for he knew the old sailor was wise and shrewd.

"You, Martin. This is not the time for you to go. You are needed here."

For a moment the boy's heart stood still. "Ole," he said in a strangled voice, "I've got to go. I want to train for a flier, help Father if he's there, be in the thick of things."

"I know," said Ole Haug, "but it needs a young head here too. See to getting the other boats out, get the other boys ready. You have planned well. You must do it again. My grandson, Knut, will be only too ready to take your place in the boat tonight, but he could not do what you can do here." He put his hand on Martin's shoulder. "It is not easy, I know that well," he said, "but these are not easy times, Martin. Each must serve where he can do it best. It looks to me that there will be many things here for you to do. You are both capable and quick-witted, and you know how to carry things through. Later will come the time for you to go."

In his heart Martin knew that his old friend was right, but in all his life he had never wanted anything so desperately as he wanted to go with those boats tonight. He stood for a long moment looking out over the blue waters of the fjord. "I'll stay," he said quietly. "And now, Ole, I'm going to see Herr Ostrander."

Ole smiled. "Give him my love," he said dryly.

Petra almost cried out in her relief when she spied her brother at last, a little way down the path. She could see that he was excited, and indeed he was too intent on tonight's venture even to notice how wet she was. "They're going, Petra! Tonight! They're going!" he told her in swift whispers. "The Holms and the Ostergaards, and what do you think—Herr Ostrander is going too!"

"Good! He's braver than we thought, I guess. Or maybe he was ashamed when you got busy so fast."

"Well, anyway, he's going, and I'm glad. He'll be more help there than he could be here. Sigurd's taking charge of one boat—"

"And you, Martin? What will your part be?" Desperately as she longed to have him stay, she had made up her mind she would not spoil his going by grieving. In times like these you had to take each situation as it came and do the best you could with it. But she could not help looking up at him anxiously.

He was still for a moment, looking straight ahead. Then he set his jaw, squared his shoulders, and looked down at her, and she had never seen his eyes look so sad. "I'm not going this time, Petra," he said. "I'll have to stay here in Norway and help. Ole Haug talked to me about it, and I know he's right." He gave a long-drawn sigh. "I guess I knew it all the time, but, oh, how I do want to go with them tonight!"

Petra nodded, her face so full of understanding that Martin felt comforted. "I know," she said. "I'd even like to go, and I'm a girl. I can imagine how hard it is for you to stay. But really I'm glad, Martin, and not just because I want you with us, either. But there's so much to be done here, and you seem to know how to go about it."

Martin's face lighted up for a moment, and then he said suddenly: "Why, you're soaking wet! One thing has to be done right now. We've got to get you home. But, Petra, I've never known you to fall in before."

Petra made the story as droll as possible, and was glad to hear him laugh as they hurried down the trail. Martin in turn told of his conversation with Ole Haug and with Herr Ostrander, and of the plans for the night's sailing.

"The boys have everything ready," he finished, "they've been waiting for this."

"And I can help, surely?"

"You can watch, close by the house, and warn us if you hear anyone starting our way."

"Otto will sleep soundly tonight, I think," said Petra, and they both chuckled.

It was nearing midnight when the boys silently gathered in the little cove above the harbor. Herr Ostrander was there, ready to set out with the others, and in the light of Martin's reasoning had agreed so readily that the boy had complimented him on his bravery. But the man had replied with a directness that surprised Martin. "It doesn't take so much courage to go as to stay, Martin. I'd say you are the brave one. Now I know the habits of those sentries. I think I can be of help in making those plans. The guard on the pier is changed at ten."

"Then toward midnight they should be getting drowsy," Martin had said calmly.

Now it was almost midnight. "Are we all here?" whispered Martin. "Count off, and see."

"One, two, three, four." The quiet count went up to twenty. How Martin longed to be one of the number! Straining their ears, the boys could hear the sentries marching back and forth—back and forth. Then came the sound of a scuffle and a hoarse shout. Martin felt suddenly sick, and his palms, as he clasped his hands in swift fear, were wet. That one shout might mean the failure of the whole venture. Supposing the boys were discovered and imprisoned! And it was he who had decided they must sail tonight!

"Crouch down!" he whispered sharply, and not an instant too soon, for on the road above the cove, two lanterns twinkled, two Nazi soldiers spoke in low tones. Martin, who understood German well, heard one say: "But I tell you I heard a shout. You would have too, if you'd had your wits about you. We've got to investigate."

"I heard it, all right," grumbled a second. "It was only one of these yokels. I know they ought to be home in bed, but we're having a tough enough time here as it is, with no one willing to so much as speak to us. If they want to get out and shout a little, I say we'd better let them alone. Come on home to bed."

"At least I'm going to use my big flashlight on the fjord," said the first. "This dark twilight up here is worse than pitch darkness. You think you see things, and then you don't. But you can't fool this big flashlight."

Martin's heart was pounding. Would that flashlight pick out any of the boys? What was happening now on the pier? He hoped fervently that Sigurd's father and Herr Dr. Ostergaard had spied the lanterns, and were keeping under cover.

Once, twice, three times that big flashlight swept the fjord. But the boats lay quietly at anchor; nothing moved on the fjord. Martin, straining his eyes anxiously toward the pier, could see no movement there.

"There, you see, everything's shipshape," said the second soldier, with a clumsy attempt at a joke. "I'm sleepy, and so is the town. What could they do here? Nothing. Come along!"

It was not until the lanterns had disappeared far up the road that anyone moved.

"That was a close call," said someone very quietly, and Martin drew a breath of relief as he recognized Herr Holm's voice.

"All clear, boys," whispered Dr. Ostergaard. "The sentries are safe till morning. Quick now. All hands to work! But quiet!"

Martin stood guard while the boats were loaded. Twice he heard far-off steps, and he almost stopped breathing, but the sounds died away. He would not have believed the work could be done with such speed and silence. They were almost ready now. He hoped he could have one final word with Sigurd.

Yes, here was Sigurd beside him. "All ready, Martin. Coming?"

Here was one last chance, and Martin almost took it. One more could find a place in the boat. But he shook Sigurd's hand and whispered: "Not this time, Sig. I want to, but I guess I can do more here right now."

For a moment Sigurd was silent, and Martin felt almost sick as he wondered if there were contempt in those blue eyes, and if his old friend were classing him with Hans Torgerson. But then Sigurd returned the handclasp. "Good boy, Martin!" he whispered. "You're needed here, that's true enough. We may have to do something about messages, you know. Listen now," he spoke quickly, "if we want to get word to you, we won't try here at Valcos—they'll be watching too closely. But my sisters are up on our summer farm on the mountaintop. You know it well, and you know how isolated it is. If there's need, we'll try to get word to them. Watch for their signal fire under the cliff— the same old signal fire we used to use. Tell Petra too. She'll be here, after you're back at school." He gave Martin's hand a quick, hard shake. "You'll be coming before long."

They were off now, feathering their oars, slipping silently down the fjord. Martin made his way as silently home, to where Petra was crouching under the hedge. Together they went up to their mother's room.

"Safely off?" she whispered softly.

"Safely off, and not a trace to incriminate anyone," Martin returned, and in swift, eager whispers told the story of the night's work, not forgetting what Sigurd had said. "But, O Mother," he finished, with a sigh, "how I did want to go with them!"

"You'll go some day, son," she answered, and reached out in the darkness to squeeze his hand. "But you did a bigger job tonight, Martin, and you'll do it again, for the boys who went, and for all Norway. There are plenty more of such jobs ahead—there's not the slightest doubt of that."

"And now our job is to watch for the signal fire," said Petra thoughtfully. "That old signal fire that always used to mean fun ahead—put now to wartime use. I wonder what the first message will be, and when it will come."

"It may tell us what our next job is to be," Martin replied.

"Yes," murmured Petra, "but maybe—just maybe —it will bring us news of Father."

IV

PETRA GOES UP THE MOUNTAIN

"PETRA! Are you almost ready?" asked Fru Engeland. "Captain Ebert and Otto left the house a few minutes ago. The others have been out for some time. I believe you could slip away now without being stopped for questions."

Petra fastened the last strap on her mountain boot and sprang to her feet, tying a deep-blue kerchief over her blond curls. "Mother, you're a treasure!" she exclaimed, giving Fru Engeland a swift, appreciative hug. "And to think we used to pet you and think you were rather timid. And now with Nazis actually quartered right here in your house, you're as brave as a lion, to say nothing of being as sharp as a tack!"

Fru Engeland smiled somewhat ruefully and shook her head. "All over Norway, for that matter, people are doing things they never expected to do," she replied. "We never considered you so resourceful either, Petra, except in ways to have fun. And now think of all the things you've been doing!" Her eyes were proud as she looked at her daughter.

45

"O Mother, I haven't done so much. Anyone would have done the same," protested Petra, looking, her mother thought, prettier than ever as she flushed at the praise. "Well, now I'll scamper off as fast as I can, for it will be a lot easier if no one sees me."

"Petra, I don't like to have you climb that mountain alone. Oh, I do wish Martin were here to go with you! You are quite sure you won't get lost?"

"I won't get lost, Mother. And this must be something important, or Inga never would have lighted her little signal fire last night. It may even be that Sigurd has found a way to send that message he spoke of. Maybe there will be word from Father." Both of them were silent for a moment, thinking longingly how welcome such word would be. "'By, now, and don't you worry," said Petra reassuringly, for her mother's face was anxious. "You know I've climbed around in these mountains ever since I was little. I won't get lost. Wish I could be here, though, to see you playing dumb when the Nazis start asking where I've gone. You're wonderful, Mother!"

Petra was laughing to help keep her mother's courage up, and her own as well. It was true that she had often climbed around the mountains, but the climb to the Holm saeter, the high mountain pasture where her friend Inga spent her summers helping her older sisters to care for the goats and cattle, was through a difficult pass where snow lay even in summer, and where it would be easy to lose one's way or slip on the steep trails. But last night Petra, watching as always, had seen Inga's signal fire high up the cliff, and had hardly been able to wait until morning to set out. Something urgent lay back of that signal, she knew very well.

She set out cautiously, for though this was one of the rare times when the Nazi officers and Otto the orderly were all absent, one or the other would be certain to turn up soon, and if they saw her so much as going out of the garden gate, there were sure to be more of those unwelcome questions. In the weeks since the Nazis had come to Valcos, she and her mother had become expert in the art of polite and vague answers to questions, a practice that was a strain on them, it was true, but far more of a strain on Captain Ebert and his staff, who found the gentle mistiness of their hostesses' conversation annoyingly hard to handle. There was no ground for complaint, and yet the captain felt that somehow he was being thwarted at every possible turn, and even outwitted at times, and he did not relish the idea.

Petra would have liked to take her rucksack with a few supplies in case it proved desirable to stay up the mountain for a while, but if she was seen leaving with a rucksack, that would bring out questions hard to evade, so she had simply tucked a package of bread and cheese into one pocket of her hiking trousers, her compass and flashlight into another, her field glasses into the big pocket of her sweater. Now, if she could just gain the woods a short distance above the house without being seen, she thought she would be fairly safe from discovery, for she was fleet of foot and well acquainted with the lower paths and their hiding places. "Whoever thought playing 'hide-and-seek' would be training for war?" she thought grimly, as she began her climb.

She had made this journey often in other years, for she and Inga were old friends, and a week or two spent at the high pastures of the Holm saeter had always been the brightest spot in her gay summers. Toward the end of her visit, the boys had always come up— Martin and the Holm boys, and, many of the young folks from neighboring saeters and from homes in the valley. Then there had been a wonderful picnic, with games and fishing and feasting and old-time folk dances, and late in the evening they had gone singing down the mountain, their voices echoing against the high cliffs across the fjord.

But never before had she made the journey alone. Father had often climbed beside her and helped her over the hard parts of the trail. And where was Father now? Not a word had come from him since the day she had taken her little sailboat down to the mouth of the fjord and warned him of the Nazis' arrival. Petra's blue eyes were anxious, and a lump came into her throat as she thought of him. Captain Ebert wanted to get hold of him, she knew well. That, they all felt sure, was the chief reason the Nazis had come to the little fishing village of Valcos. They wanted Captain Engeland and his big boat, and the smaller fishing craft. They wanted supplies too, of course, and had already begun systematically pillaging the village and countryside. Well, that was bad enough, but they shouldn't have Father! And they shouldn't have all the fishing boats, either. Already half a dozen, at least, had slipped out of Valcos, loaded with Norwegian men and boys on their way to England. That was a satisfaction! But there was anxiety connected with it, too, for so far no word had come of their safe arrival. Could it possibly be that Inga had heard something about the boats, Petra wondered. She had something important to tell, that was sure.

The morning was fresh and bright, and Petra, in spite of her worries, had a feeling of freedom and light-heartedness. At least there were no Nazis lurking in unexpected corners up here, watching, waiting, ready at any moment to pounce with their questions. She drew a deep breath of the clear mountain air and walked faster. But then her foot slipped a little on an icy spot in the trail, and she went on more carefully, so anxious to reach the top that it was difficult to hold herself back.

The hardest part of the trail, the Valcos pass, lay ahead. That was narrow and treacherous. The snow would still be piled there, and a steep precipice plunged into the valley far below. Well, she could make it. She had to. She was almost there. She braced herself for the hazardous climb, and then stopped in sudden alarm. Could it be that she had heard voices high above her, away up the pass? Sounds carried, she knew, with surprising distinctness through these passes. It might even be someone on the mountain-top. She certainly had not expected to meet anyone on the little-used trail today.

But the past weeks had taught her caution, and she looked swiftly about for a hiding place. A few yards ahead, slightly to one side of the trail, were some large rocks. She sped toward them and crouched down in their shelter. She was not a moment too soon. There could be no mistake about it now. The voices were coming nearer and Petra's heart seemed to turn over as she listened, for the strangers were talking in German, and there was something hauntingly familiar about one of the voices. She understood German fairly well, but the men were talking in low tones, and she had to strain to catch the words.

"You know their value to us, and even more to the Norwegians. Are you sure they will be safe, hidden in these mountains?" one said dubiously. "They will have to be carefully guarded, of course."

"Oh, I suppose a light guard will be advisable, though no one would think of suspecting anything of the kind. The Norwegians are trusting souls, and anyway we're keeping them too busy these days and too well watched for them to be roaming the mountains."

"You're sure you know some well-hidden caves, eh?"

"Absolutely. Why, I hiked and hunted in these mountains when I was a boy, and I know the caves and hiding places like a book. I can easily make you a map. And we must get this business out of the way to be ready for a bigger job ahead."

Where had she heard that voice before? It went way back into her early childhood, she knew that. Then from her hiding place she caught a glimpse of the men as they came around the bend, and now indeed she felt almost stunned, for one of the men, a tall, fair-haired chap, was Kurt Nagler, who had come as a little German refugee lad after the last war to be cared for and brought up in her Grandfather Engeland's home. Many a time Kurt had carried her on his back up this very pass. Many a time he had taken Martin on hunting trips through these mountains. In late years, they had not seen him often, for Grandfather had established him as partner in a hardware store in the town of Halven, where Martin's school was. But now and then he had come for dinner on a week-end evening, sailing up the fjord with Martin.

Some months ago he had gone away, just for a little vacation, he had said, and one of the men with him now, Julius Staeck, had taken charge of the store. Julius was small and insignificant in appearance, and surly and short in manner. Her father said that he was doing the business no good, and that it would be well if Kurt cut his vacation short and hurried home.

Now Kurt had come home, but Petra wished with all her heart that he had stayed away. She had heard stories of how German refugees, cared for and brought up in Norway after the last war, had come back now, in Norway's trouble, to give aid to the invaders. But Kurt, who had stayed right here, who had been one of them—she never would have believed this of him, if she had not heard it with her own ears.

The third man was dark and stocky and limped a little, though he could keep up with the others in spite of that. He was talking now, too low for her to catch all he said, but he spoke with authority and seemed to be in charge. Someone or something was to be hidden in these mountains—so much was clear enough. As they passed her hiding place, she heard him say: "We shall need a map, and a good one, for none of us but you are familiar with these mountains, and it would be too risky to use you as a guide. They would know you at once if you were seen, and your usefulness would be at an end. And bigger work lies ahead for you."

Her heart was heavy as the voices died away and she went on up the trail. It was hard to accustom herself to seeing her old friend Kurt in this new light. And after all she had really heard so little. There was little she could do about it. She could manage, perhaps, in some way to have Kurt watched, but it was plain he was proceeding with great caution. What could they learn in that way? Wait a minute, though—it might be that Inga knew something about this. That might have been the reason for the signal. She must hurry now. She must get there with all speed.

She was in the pass now, and the going was much harder. She tried to get control of her seething thoughts. She must take no chances of losing her footing and sliding down that plunging precipice. She hadn't remembered that the path was so steep, the footholds so precarious. Oh, if only she were not all alone! "But I'd better just be thankful," she told herself, "that it wasn't here I heard those voices. I'd have had a time scrambling out of sight to safety here. And seems to me I've just heard something awfully important."

She paused for a moment to take stock of what lay directly ahead. What she saw made her give a cry of delight, for coming briskly toward her down the trail was sure-footed Inga, well used to these trails and not a bit afraid of them.

"O Inga, I'm glad to see you!" she cried. "This trail—"

"I know, and I was taking no chances," returned Inga smiling, though her eyes were anxious. "We need you, Petra. Just wait till you hear what's going on up here. We need someone with quick wits like you." She stopped smiling and looked around suddenly, as if more than half afraid of being overheard. "We know we need someone who can speak German, and we hope we're going to need someone who can speak English."

"German!" echoed Petra. "Then maybe I have some idea what this is all about. But, O Inga, I had thought I would be away from that language, for today, at least!"

"I'm afraid you're not. And you must stay more than today," said Inga urgently. "Tonight is when we are going to need you most, I think. Or maybe tomorrow night. I can't quite tell. O Petra!" For a minute Petra thought her usually lighthearted friend was going to cry, but she controlled herself and went on: "Something very bad, and we think very important, is happening up here in these mountains. And the trouble is, we don't know what it is. We don't understand it at all."

"Let's not talk about it now," warned Petra in a low tone, "not until we're safe in the cabin." And Inga nodded a ready assent.

Once inside the log cabin, with the thick door shut and bolted, both girls talked at once, with golden-haired Margot, and dark-eyed Karen, the two older sisters, joining in eagerly. Then, in spite of themselves, they laughed. "One at a time," ordered Margot.

"You start, Margot. You're the oldest and certainly the most sensible," said Petra.

"Well, what I have to say doesn't take so long to tell," said Margot. "Here is the story, Petra. You know how long one may roam around up here, caring for the cows and goats, without seeing anyone. All summer, perhaps, except for the few other girls in the neighboring saeters, doing the same job as we."

"We never see strangers up here," burst in Inga, who could contain herself no longer. "But day before yesterday, Petra, when I was out hunting some cows that had strayed, I saw two men down the other side of the mountain."

"What did they look like?" Petra interrupted eagerly.

"They were quite a ways away, but one was short and thin, and the other was stocky and limped a little. I'm sure they didn't want to be seen, for they vanished so quickly after I came in sight—you know it is easy to disappear up here where there are so many rocks and trees—"

"And caves?" interrupted Petra again.

"Yes, why do you say that? These mountains have many caves, of course."

"I know, but go on—"

"Well, that seemed queer enough, but yesterday, when I was off in still another direction, after some of the goats, I caught sight of the men again. This time

I'm sure they didn't see me, for I was the one who was careful to hide quickly. I wanted to see what they were about. And they were exploring with the greatest care you ever saw, going in and out among the rocks and the boulders and everywhere. I thought they were looking for something they had lost, and at last they went away. But I'm afraid they'll be back, and I'm sure they are up to troublemaking—they were taking such care not to be seen. And I thought—" Inga paused and looked as if she weren't sure of being believed— "I thought they were talking German. But of course I don't know much German. So we wanted to send for you, but we knew it wouldn't be easy for you to get away, and we thought we would wait another day, but we didn't see any more of them—"

"And then," Karen interrupted, "last night a plane came over. It circled and swooped quite low. We couldn't tell for sure, but we were afraid it was German. We saw something fall from it, down the mountain a ways. You know how light it stays up here these nights. Inga ran down to see if she could find what it was."

"This is what I found," said Inga, "this note, tied to a stone to weight it. It's written in Norwegian, but it doesn't seem to be meant for us. It hasn't any greeting or any signature. And the writing is so queer—as if it was written by someone who didn't know Norwegian and was trying to write at someone's dictation. See, what do you think of it, Petra?"

Petra, examining the note, was as puzzled as the others. For written in jerky, uncertain letters, were simply the words: "Can't land tonight. Back tomorrow night at ten. Try to guide us to a safe landing in some meadow."

"That was when we decided not to wait, but to send down the old signal in hopes you would see it and be able to break away and come," said Inga. "Because, on the other side, is a little message that I think is written in German."

Petra turned the strange note over, and found three words, written in the same jerky style, as though the writer was not familiar with German, either. The words were simply, "Be very careful."

"Then it wasn't Sigurd who told you to send the message down," said Petra, in some disappointment.

"Sigurd!" cried all three in amazement. "What made you think of that?" added Margot.

"Oh, of course, you don't know," said Petra, and quickly explained the new use to which they hoped to put the old signal.

"I only wish we had heard from Sigurd," said Inga with a sigh. "No, this signal was our own idea."

"Well, all this may fit in pretty well with something that happened on my way up here," said Petra, and told her story in a few words. "This message may have been intended for those men, of course, from some Nazi," she said, "or it may be for you, from someone English."

"If it was intended for them, they don't know that the plane intends to return tonight, or they wouldn't have gone away. On the other hand, they may be afraid to stay around here longer, for fear of discovery," said Inga.

"If it was intended for you, and if it's from a friend, is there any place a plane could land up here?" asked Petra.

"Yes, the south pasture up here on the plateau would be a good place," returned Margot. "We figured that out without much trouble."

"Well, this is what I think we had better do," said Petra, after a few moments' thought. "We will keep a sharp lookout for the plane. Martin has taught me to spot some of the English ones, and some of the German ones too. We must have lanterns ready, and if I can recognize it as an English plane, we will try to guide them to a safe landing with lanterns."

"But what if it's German? What if it's for those men?" asked Karen, her dark eyes anxious. "What if we make a mistake and guide Germans down? They might shoot us if they thought we knew too much."

"Yes, there's that chance, all right. Do you have guns up here?" asked Petra slowly.

"Yes, you know the boys leave their guns up here for hunting," answered Margot. "We know how to use them too," she added firmly, "and we can do it if necessary." The others nodded gravely, but Karen was whiter than ever.

"We'll have to be ready," said Petra, "but I have an idea, girls, that that plane is not going to be German. I have an idea that it is English, and the note was written in Norwegian to throw anyone off the scent if it got into the wrong hands. It might even be from someone who knows Sigurd, or—" she hesitated— "or Father. It would have to be something of great importance to make one plane willing to land in occupied territory, where Nazi soldiers are not far off."

"Oh, ten o'clock is so long to wait!" said Inga, with a little shiver.

"But we have a great deal to do," Margot reminded them. "We must get the cows in early, and prepare food in case the fliers are friends and need it. We must get lanterns ready."

"Oh, I wish we could get some real help here—Father or Uncle Charles," burst out Karen, who wanted to sound brave and matter-of-fact like the others, but found the situation very terrifying.

"But they are at the other farm up the valley. We have no way of reaching them. We have to handle this ourselves," said Margot, with determination.

"We can do it," said Petra firmly. "I know that now. Whatever we have to do, we can do. I've found that out. Come now, let's get at it. There's plenty to do. And by ten o'clock we must be ready."

The Plane Comes Over

EVEN AT TEN O'CLOCK it was not entirely dark on the Norwegian mountaintop where the four girls waited, tense and alert, for the promised appearance of the plane. Everything was ready. Petra had planned a way to guide the plane to a safe landing. Margot and Karen and Inga had an abundance of food ready—milk and cheese and newly baked rye bread and *lefse*, and freshly churned butter. The saeter cabin was scrubbed and shining. They were ready for all emergencies. But it seemed there was to be no emergency. Ten minutes passed, fifteen, twenty, and no plane appeared. All day they had been waiting in great suspense for this moment. And now the moment had arrived, and nothing happened.

Petra broke the silence at last. "It may be that it was a German plane that flew over last night. It may be that the note was intended for the men I almost met on the trail—the men Inga saw prowling around the mountainside. Perhaps the ones in the plane found that out, and aren't coming back tonight."

"Yes, but the more I think of it, the more I don't believe that was a German plane," began Inga, when a low hum was heard in the distance—a hum that grew into a roar.

"There it is! There it is!" cried Margot, and Karen gave a frightened glance at their brothers' guns, set ready in case of need.

"I can't fire one of those," she whispered. "I just couldn't do it."

Petra, who was looking intently at the plane through her field glasses, gave a low cry of joy. "It's English! It's English! We don't need the guns! We need the lanterns! It is just barely light enough for me to distinguish the markings on the plane. It won't be light enough for them to land without help."

"Not in unfamiliar territory, anyway," said Inga. "Or, look, is the territory unfamiliar? Look, they are heading straight for the south pasture, where we're going."

Indeed, the plane was there before they were, circling slowly overhead.

Petra's plan was simple enough. They would just run round and round the field with their lanterns, outlining with a circle of light the safe area for landing. It worked easily and well, and the plane began to descend.

Petra's heart pounded as she watched. Though her brother Martin had spent some time teaching her to distinguish planes, she had had almost no actual experience in doing it, and in the twilight it would have been entirely possible for her to make a mistake. What if they were helping enemies to land? Supposing her plan was putting them all in danger!

But a shriek of delight from Inga sent all doubts flying, "Sigurd! Sigurd! Sigurd!" she was crying, racing over the pasture with her arms outstretched. "O Sigurd!"

It was Sigurd, sure enough, running toward them, while another boy, smiling a little shyly, was walking in their direction, a boy whom Sigurd introduced to them as Ruggles Swift, an English pilot.

Then the English boy was made welcome too, and soon all of them were in the safe shelter of the saeter cabin, the boys heartily enjoying their meal while Inga stood guard, drawing the thick homespun window curtain aside the merest trifle, in the unlikely event of their being surprised. While he was eating his supper, Sigurd swiftly told the story.

Yes, the first two boatloads of boys and men from Valcos had had a fair enough voyage and landed safely in England. It wasn't easy, of course, in the open boats, and it had taken longer than they had planned, for there had been a storm. But they had weathered it, and they had been welcomed in England and were in training right now. He himself was to become a flier, like Ruggles here.

"But isn't it terribly dangerous for you to be here, Sigurd?" asked Karen anxiously.

"Well, it isn't exactly the safest thing I could do. We must talk and plan fast, and get off as quickly as we can."

"And Father—have you heard anything of him?" asked Petra, half afraid to ask the question, yet feeling that she must know. "Do you know if he is in England?"

"Oh, yes. He is there. Indeed he is. And he got his big boat over. He is the one who is chiefly responsible for our being here right now. He needed a way to communicate with folks here, and I suggested our saeter, as I had planned with Martin. He sent love to you all, and you are not to worry about him."

"But what is he doing?" persisted Petra. "Something very dangerous?"

"Wait till I'm through, and you'll know as much about it as I do, which isn't a great deal at that. It is something of a secret and confidential nature, and very important."

Petra nodded. Father would be a valuable man in work of that kind. He knew how to be daring and cautious at the same time, and his judgment was always good. But Sigurd was rushing on with his story, and she gave him her whole attention, for his voice was urgent, and it was plain that there was work ahead for all of them.

"You know we all thought that the main business of the Nazis in Valcos was to try to get hold of the boats—the fishing fleet, and especially Petra's father and his big boat. But Captain Engeland has found that that is only part of it. They are planning to use this as a base for certain operations. They have some other plans as well, we think, but so far we haven't been able to find out anything at all definite."

"I heard them talking of hiding things in the mountains!" cried Petra. "That must be part of it. And they did speak of a big job ahead," she added thoughtfully.

"But how can they use it as a base? There's no means of fast transportation—no good roads—and the mountains are right behind the town, and steep," said Margot.

"Do you forget the fjord? Transportation on that isn't very fast, maybe, but it's pretty dependable. And the Germans know there are such things as planes, don't forget. They may have some possible landing fields spotted. For instance, you saw us come in tonight and land safely in the south pasture. German planes could do the same, though I'll admit they wouldn't have the same guiding lights." Sigurd laughed heartily as he thought of the girls running pell-mell around the field with their lanterns, and the other boy joined him, for he understood from Sigurd's motions what he was talking about. "Who thought that plan up?"

"Petra! You might know!" chuckled Inga. "Petra's always had a fertile brain to think up the unexpected. You know she was always thinking up a new twist to our games."

Sigurd nodded. He remembered well how often he had been amused in the past to watch his young sister and her friends at their games, and to see Petra stop suddenly in the midst of things and bring out an idea which doubled the hilarity. "I guess Petra's proved that she can use her quick wits in other ways than games these last weeks," he agreed, "and it looks as if there'd be plenty more chances for her right ahead."

"Somebody certainly had his wits about him when that note was written and dropped," said Petra. "You didn't explain that."

"Oh, that!" Sigurd laughed. "That was my friend Ruggles here." The English boy laughed too, for Sigurd's odd pronunciation of his name entertained him hugely. "Ruggles here is trying to teach me English; and I'm trying to teach him Norwegian, but he can't help laughing at some of my pronunciation and I guess I laugh at him too, so we're even. Well, he had spied some men on the mountain when we were reconnoitering, and I—" he hesitated and glanced at Petra as though he didn't like to go on,—"I recognized one as Kurt Nagler, I thought."

"Yes, I know," Petra assured him. "I saw them myself. It just doesn't seem possible, but I heard them planning, so I know it is. I've heard of other refugees, but Kurt—I surely didn't think it of him."

Her voice trembled a little, and Sigurd said gently: "All over Norway people are feeling just as you do. Don't take it too much to heart, Petra. After all, it isn't as if one of our own people had turned traitor." He paused for a moment, and then resumed briskly: "We wanted to drop you girls a note, but we thought it entirely possible it might land some ways down the mountain and be picked up by Kurt and his friends. That's why there was no salutation and no signature. We wanted to give no clues. That's why I didn't even dare write it myself, for I once did some work for Kurt in his store, and he might have recognized my writing. We didn't want them to know I was in this, for then they'd know that someone who knew the terrain was on to them. We want them to go ahead with what they are doing, because we think that with your help we can spoil their game."

"I think so too," said Petra eagerly. "I've been thinking something out but go on and finish your story, Sig."

"Well, you see, we wanted them to think this was just an English plane on a more or less routine re-connoitering flight if they saw it at all. If they knew I was in it, they'd be pretty sure we had business with them right here, and be on their guard. So Rug wrote the note, and it was hard for him to get the Norwegian words as I dictated them. That's why it looked so jerky."

"We had something like that figured out," said golden-haired Margot, smiling at Ruggles so brightly that he immediately resolved to work much harder at his Norwegian so that next time he came over he could talk to her a little himself. "But why the German words?"

"Oh!" Sigurd laughed again. "That was just to mix those guys up in case they picked up the note instead of you. We hoped it might scare them away. We didn't like them hanging around the saeter here." He pushed his plate away. "Did that good old Norwegian cooking hit the spot!" he declared. "Now listen carefully!" As if they were not! "Petra's father has reason to believe that the Nazis are storing ammunition around here in the mountains above Valcos—guns that have been confiscated from the Norwegians, he thinks.

Apparently they feel that it is a very safe place, since Valcos is a small settlement at best, and already a good many of its men and boys have left. And of course these mountains are wild, and there are many caves."

"That's what those men were doing!" cried Inga. "They were searching for hiding places! How could they know I'd be out on the mountain, hunting some lost goats?"

"Undoubtedly that is just what they were doing. I surely hope they didn't see you. For one thing, we don't want them to know we suspect what is going on. And for another, they wouldn't hesitate to shoot if they thought you were making any discoveries. And anyway," he added grimly, "they'll be commandeering our cattle and goats before long, I'm afraid, so you needn't take any risks in hunting them up and keeping the herd together."

"We'll keep some of them hidden, then," said Margot with spirit. "I know a pasture in the woods where I can drive some of them tomorrow, and I'll do it."

"Good girl!" nodded Sigurd. "That's the spirit! Now, the big question is this: how are we to find out where they are hiding this ammunition? We must find it, if we can possibly do so, and we must spirit it away. If only we could keep the plane here and circle around the mountain but of course that is out of the question."

"Listen to this!" said Petra, who had been thinking intently even as she listened. "As they passed me on the trail, I heard Kurt saying that he would make them a map. He said he used to hunt and hike up here, and knew these mountains like a book."

"He said that?" cried Sigurd. "That gives me an idea. Do you remember how he used to take Martin up here hunting? He may have in mind some of the caves where they used to take shelter. Martin would know them well, Petra. When will he be home?"

"I don't know. All weekend leaves from Halven have been canceled by the Nazis."

Sigurd hesitated, dreading to make the suggestion that he felt he must make. But Petra understood as well as he did what was necessary, and she was the one who spoke. "You want me to get the word to Martin," she said quietly, and thought for a moment. "Yes, I think I can promise that. At least I can try. And another thing," she went on, "we really ought to have Kurt's map."

"It would certainly be a good thing," agreed Sigurd. "But that would be taking too great a risk, I'm afraid. I think Martin would have a good idea where those caves might be. Kurt would naturally guide them to the best ones—he wouldn't ever dream that we'd be roaming the mountains these days. They think they've taken all our guns—" he grinned as he looked at the ones stacked in the corner—"though plenty are hidden all over Norway. Better hide those with care," he warned, "you may need them."

"Yes, they wouldn't expect anyone to be hunting in the mountains these days," agreed Petra. "And they are keeping such close guard over people, the men especially, that they would never think anyone might discover something hidden in those caves. Now if we can get that information, how do we get it to you? It wouldn't be safe for you to make many trips like this. Already you've come twice."

"We'll try to make one more—let's see—would next Monday be too soon?"

Petra thought fast. "I think we can manage. There's no time to waste, I know. I must have time to get to Martin, and he must have time to do what he has to do. We are watched so very closely now that we'll have to be extremely careful or the whole thing will fall through. I manage to get away once in a while, because they think I'm a harmless sort of nitwit, and I always bring some dainties back for the officers."

They all laughed at this, but Sigurd was back to business at once. "A week from tonight then. And now it is high time we were on our way back."

"And if you can't get back here, what shall we do then?" asked Petra anxiously.

"I'll have to leave that to you," said Sigurd, rising and looking down at her with serious eyes that yet held a confident smile. "To you and Martin. You know how important this is, and so do we. We'll do our best to be back, but would you like to know what your father said? He said: 'Petra and Martin have already proved what they can do. We can leave it to them if necessary.'"

"Did Father say that?" cried Petra, her blue eyes very bright. "We won't fail!"

"Sigurd!" whispered Inga in alarm. "I think I see someone coming up the trail. Go quick! Hurry! Hurry!"

Without a word the boys slipped swiftly out of the little back door and over the field.

"Can it really be someone at this hour?" asked Margot, going to Inga's side. "Not just a stray cow or—yes, you're right!" She drew in her breath sharply.

"Maybe it's just one of the neighbors," said Karen, trying to sound brave. "One of the Aronsens, maybe." But a glance out of the window crushed that theory.

"Girls, if it's anyone—one of the Nazis—" said Petra swiftly, "let me do the talking. I'm kind of used to them." She was straining her ears for the first sputtering sound of the airplane engine. Oh, if only the boys could get away before anyone came!

"Oh, I wish the boys would hurry," said Karen in a stifled voice. "Why are they so slow? Do you suppose someone has stopped them?"

"They'll get started," said Petra, forcing herself to sound steady, but her face was as white as the others'. "It just seems slow to us because we're so anxious. Here, we mustn't all stand so near the window. I'll watch. You put things away. We must get these dishes out of sight. And hide those guns! But keep one where we can use it if we have to!"

"He's coming to the cabin, whoever it is," said Margot, as the three sisters rushed to get things under cover. "Oh, if only the boys can get away!"

VI

An Uninvited Guest at the Saeter

P ETRA, FROM HER POST near the window, whispered: "Hurry, hurry, girls! He's almost here! Is everything out of sight?"

Inga whisked the telltale supper dishes of the boys out of sight, and Margot whispered in desperation: "I don't know where to hide the guns. And no one must find those here! Oh, why don't Sigurd and Ruggles get started! If we could only hear their airplane starting!"

"Here," said Karen almost inaudibly, and opened a small secret recess under the back window, where things were sometimes stored for winter, "hide the guns here."

"Oh, of course!" Swiftly Margot shoved the guns into the recess, all except one which she slipped onto the little shelf under the table beside which she now took her stand.

"Don't use it, Margot, unless it is absolutely necessary," whispered Petra. "It would get us into terribly serious trouble."

Hardly had she spoken when there was a chorused sigh of relief through the little cabin, for the noisy

71

sound of a starting airplane engine was heard, then a steady throb. "They're off," breathed Karen, and the girls looked at each other almost weak with the sudden break in tension.

"I don't suppose it was half so long as it seemed to us," murmured Inga. "And they didn't even know what danger they were in."

"It isn't over yet," said Petra grimly. A moment later there came a pounding at their door.

The Holm girls had had no experience with Nazis, and they sent a look of agonized appeal to Petra. She straightened her shoulders—a gesture she had used many times these past weeks—went to the door and opened it just a crack, thankful to know that Margot, behind her at the table, had a gun ready to her hand in case of absolute need.

To her great surprise it was the lame man she had seen earlier that day on the mountain who was standing there, and he had his cap in his hand and was smiling. "I am sorry to trouble you young ladies at such an hour," he said apologetically in excellent Norwegian, "but I thought I heard a plane and I hoped you could tell me about it. I was hoping I could get a lift to Oslo, perhaps. I have got myself lost in the mountains, and, as you can see, I am greatly handicapped."

"I am sorry. I'm afraid we can't tell you much about a plane," said Petra, taking her cue from his own extreme politeness. "Planes do sometimes go over, of course. I believe there were one or two over this evening. Did you notice, Margot?"

Margot was getting her poise back now, and she in turn took her cue from Petra. "Yes, I think you're right," she agreed, and added, "German planes fly over now and then. Sometimes they even land near by and let off one or two people for some special reasons, I suppose, and then take off again. We've even fed several people who've been let off somewhere in the neighborhood and then gone down the trail somewhere." All of which, Petra knew from the girls' earlier accounts, was strictly true.

She wanted to hug Margot for following her lead with such satisfying completeness. But now she saw that the man was looking at her searchingly. "Aren't you quite a way from home, young lady?" he asked. "I believe I've seen you in Valcos. Is it safe for you to be so far away from home in these troubled times?"

Petra's heart was pounding, for she was far from wishing to be discovered up here, and she knew well enough that a threat lay behind those quiet words. She would have hard work to explain her presence here in case Captain Ebert found out about the plane and began to ask questions. When had this man seen her in Valcos? Was he only trying to frighten her, or had he really been hidden somewhere there by Kurt? Was he letting her know that he was alert to what was going on in her village and its immediate surroundings?

She thought fast and, though she was thoroughly frightened, she managed to answer firmly: "I came up here hoping I could get some butter and a special kind of fine cheese for the officers quartered in our house.

Captain Ebert is very kind in allowing me to go from home for needed supplies."

The man's next speech almost threw them off their guard, it was so strongly in contrast with his former politeness. "Where are those fliers?" he demanded harshly. "Someone has been here this evening. You are hiding someone."

"Fliers!" echoed Petra in a bewildered tone. "I'm sure I don't know at all." Which fortunately, she thought, was the exact truth. "We are hiding no one." And the other girls, when he turned to them, managed to sound—and without great effort—quite as bewildered as she.

"Stand aside! I demand to search this hovel," said the man with a contemptuous glance about the neat and cheerful little room.

Silently Petra stood aside, knowing well enough that she could do nothing else.

There was only one other room, a sort of dairy and cook-room where the milk was cared for and the cheeses were made, and where an extra cot or two stood ready for emergency use. It was in its usual spick-and-span condition, and certainly there was nothing suspicious to be seen there. The man looked dissatisfied and out of temper as he came back into the main room. Then apparently he had another idea, for a triumphant smile came over his face. The beds! Perhaps they had hidden someone in those deep, old-fashioned beds. He poked his cane into the thick feather beds, looking so disgruntled when he found nothing there that Petra, frightened as she was, had to stifle a hysterical giggle.

"No one seems to be here," the man muttered, half to himself. "I may have been wrong about their hiding anyone, but there was a plane around here this evening, I know that much. I heard it take off."

"Planes do land around here sometimes, especially if they are in trouble, or perhaps they want to let off passengers, as Margot said," Petra said, anxious to soothe his ruffled feelings. "You see, there aren't many places where they can land around here—only a few meadows and plateaus." She was trying to think of some way to get rid of this unwelcome visitor as quickly as possible and without an actual clash. She was thinking of that secret recess where the guns were hidden. No one would suspect it of being there, it fitted so naturally into the little dwelling, but she felt she would breathe much more freely when this thorough searcher was off the place.

Margot's mention of feeding plane passengers came to her aid, and now she made the polite and practical suggestion: "If you have been wandering around the mountain, lost, no doubt you are hungry, and it is all the more necessary for you to have food since you have been disappointed in the hope you had of getting quickly to Oslo. We could prepare a lunch for you to take with you in your pocket, if you like. And we could give you a little plan of the trail."

The man gave her a quick, shrewd glance, but she looked so small and so guileless that he said, in a milder tone, "Well, a sandwich or two wouldn't go amiss, I'll admit."

Never was a lunch prepared with more dispatch, and when the door was closed, and their surprise visitor was disappearing down the trail, Margot said, with a deep-drawn sigh: "I see now why Sigurd had so much confidence in you, Petra. It seemed queer to me at the time. After all, you're only fourteen."

"Sometimes I feel like four hundred," said Petra, smiling a trifle unsteadily. "You don't know yet what it's like to have Nazis quartered in your home, trying to find out about your father, your boats, watching everything. I guess I grew up the first hour they were there. But you didn't do so badly yourself, Margot, and the others too. And oh, how wonderful that the boys got away!" she added briskly. "That was thanks to Inga's sharp eyes."

"Petra!" said Inga anxiously. "I wish he hadn't seen you up here. It certainly isn't going to make it any easier for you to get to Martin."

"I know that well enough," replied Petra. "But I've got to do it. You heard what Father said to Sigurd. And, anyway, I'd have to do it."

"Well," responded Inga, "I suppose you'll have to try, anyway."

"Try!" echoed Petra. "I've got to *do* it! Trying isn't good enough. I've got to get word to Martin, and then together we've got to find out about those munition dumps, and then we've got to see that the word gets back to Father."

"Petra!" burst out Margot. "I can't bear to have you set out on anything like that. They didn't know this man was around here now and might well be spying on you. They didn't know quite how dangerous it would be."

"I can avoid the man, I think. I did it this morning. I've had enough training so my ears are pretty sharp," returned Petra, "and, anyway, I have a right to be on my way home. But I do have to change my plans, that's sure. When I was talking to Sigurd I was planning to go on a fishing jaunt down the fjord and get to Martin that way. I did that once, and got word safely through to Father, but that was right at the beginning, and I don't believe I can risk that again, especially if the lame man is around Valcos. He will be suspicious of me, and he'll be watching."

"How on earth are you going to manage, then?" demanded Inga.

"I'll have to take that short cut over the mountain— the way Martin comes home when he's in a hurry and doesn't want to be observed."

"Oh, but Petra! That's a hard trail even for Martin. And won't they see you leaving home for that as well as they would if you sailed down the fjord?"

"No," returned Petra, and it was evident that her mind was intent on some plan, "because, you see, I shan't go home first. I shall go directly to Martin from here."

"Oh, you can't, Petra!" exclaimed Margot, feeling that as the oldest of the group she couldn't allow Petra to take such a risk. "You don't even know where those trails connect, and these mountains of ours aren't anything to play with. You know even experienced old mountain climbers sometimes get into trouble here."

"I know all that," admitted Petra. "I've thought it all over. But I'll just have to do it, I guess. Looks as if it's my only chance. I'm afraid they'll be watching me and not allowing me even the little freedom I've had. I'm afraid that lame man is suspicious and that he's going to warn them."

"Petra's right," said Inga, with a vigorous nod. "Only, Petra, I'm going with you. I'm much more used to these mountains than you are."

Petra shook her head, though it was plain the idea was very appealing. "No, for if they discovered our absence, there would be two to account for instead of one, and they'd feel more convinced than ever that we are up to something. No, I have my compass, and you can make me a map, and I'll be awfully careful. I'm sure I can make it—I just have to. Tomorrow morning, bright and early, I'll start out. Don't forget to give me the cheese for Captain Ebert. That's my talking point."

"And a strong one," said Inga, bringing out the pun so unexpectedly that they all laughed, though somewhat shakily.

"And if they come here looking for you, what are we to say?" asked Karen.

"You must simply tell them I set out and must have got lost in the mountains on my way home. I only hope," she added, with her old flashing smile, "that you will not be right."

Though it was very early, the sun was already high over the mountain when Petra said good-by the next morning. Margot tucked Captain Ebert's cheese and butter, and a substantial lunch for Petra, into a little rucksack which she settled on her young friend's back. "Now you are not going to starve on the way, at least," she said. "Eat the captain's cheese if you get too hungry." Both girls laughed, for they were determined to make the parting cheerful. They were not allowing themselves to think of the dangers ahead.

Petra had said good-by to Karen out in the little fenced enclosure where she was already busy at the morning milking. "But where is Inga?" she asked, unwilling to leave without saying farewell to her friend, yet knowing well that she could waste no time in waiting.

"Inga is rounding up some of the goats to drive them to the higher pasture in the woods, just in case the Nazis came around commandeering the live-stock, as Sigurd warned us," said Margot, looking somewhat anxiously toward the woods. "I guess the fact of the matter was she couldn't bear to see you start off alone. She was really worried about that."

"Well, please tell her good-by from me, then," said Petra. "I mustn't wait, I guess. Tell her I'll be very careful, and I'll use the map she gave me of where the trail divides, and I'll use my compass and take every precaution."

"I hope Captain Ebert will like his cheese so well he'll send you back for more," said Margot. "And tell him we have other varieties in case this doesn't suit." And both girls were smiling as Petra set off down the trail.

This morning was as bright as yesterday's, but the feeling of freedom Petra had then was not with her today. Sigurd and Ruggles—would they get the news to her father in England? Then how would they get later word to Father—word that he wanted and needed? It wouldn't be safe for the boys to fly back after what happened last night. They had narrowly escaped this time, and she was sure the Nazis were suspicious and would be watching for them. They must find some way to warn them not to land again. Why hadn't they thought of that before she left the Holm saeter? It might be impossible for her to get word of that back to the girls. But no, she thought, straightening her shoulders with a determined air, they just couldn't admit that anything was impossible these days.

But now the trail was growing so difficult that she had to give it her full attention. If she put her foot just there, and held tight to the branch above, she could get over that narrow bit where the snow lay deep and there was almost no sure footing, and the precipice fell sharply away. What if she couldn't make that dangerous journey to Martin? This was bad enough, but when she came to that treacherous pass that joined the two trails, could she find her way? Oh, if only someone were with her! If only she were not all alone! The mountains were bleak and terrifying. She wished with all her heart that she had not refused Inga's urgent request so decidedly. Enemies might be lurking anywhere—she had found that out yesterday. Alone, she might not get through. A sound caught her ear, and her heart stood still. Someone was not far off. She listened again. Yes, that was a hurriedly stifled cough!

She was over that bad bit of trail now, and she looked wildly about for some kind of hiding place—any kind. Not far away was what looked like a shallow cave, and she ducked hastily into it, holding her hand over her mouth to still the sound of her swift, frightened breathing.

For a moment she sat there tense and still, hoping to give the other person on the trail time to get well ahead of her, if he were going in that direction, or to pass her if he were climbing upward. But no one passed her on the trail. And then her ear caught a faint sound close at hand. Suddenly she knew that she was not alone in the cave.

VII

THE CAVE ON THE LOST TRAIL

T HE OTHER OCCUPANT of the cave was as quiet as Petra, and evidently as anxious not to be discovered. Perhaps she could slip out as quickly as she had come in.

She began to edge toward the opening and had almost reached it when a hand was laid on her arm. She gave a sharp cry, and then, in an onrush of relief that left her almost faint, she gasped: "Inga! What are you doing here? Never in all my life was I so glad to see anyone!"

"I knew you would be," replied Inga, "so when you wouldn't let me come, I just came anyway. This is no job for one alone. I left a note for Margot under the milk pans," she added, "so don't worry." Her face was as white as Petra's, and she said: "I was as scared as you were. I didn't expect you along so soon, and I was afraid it was—"

"I know," said Petra quickly, "the lame man or one of his crew. And what's more, they may not be so far away. That's why I wanted to get started so early. I hoped I'd get the first start. But someone," she added, smiling a little as they set off down the trail, "got ahead

82

of me. I always knew you were a determined individual, but I didn't expect this."

"Well, I'm at least going to get you over that part of
the trail that connects with the one to Martin. I'm sure
I know the way—I may even know a short cut. And I
don't believe you've ever gone over that trail, have you?"

"That's right, I haven't. I'm much better on the
fjord than in the mountains, but with an expert old
mountaineer like you," she said, smiling broadly now,
"we'll be there in no time."

"And yet you wanted to come alone," scolded Inga,
"and I dare say you'd have made it, at that, but you
might have had a pretty tough time."

Even the Valcos Pass didn't seem so terrifying
with Inga there to go ahead, to give a steadying hand
now and then, to point out danger spots and offer en-
couragement. Inga knew these trails well. "The mountains are safe enough if you just stick to the trails and
watch your step," she said, pleased that they were
making such good time.

But when they reached the point where one trail
forked down toward Valcos, another angled off down
the other side of the mountain, and still a third led
through a steep pass, Inga stood for some time, her
gray eyes serious as she considered the situation.
"We've always taken the Valcos fork here, of course,
and I'd forgotten there were three trails meeting
here—I thought there were just two."

"One isn't very well outlined—that's probably
why," said Petra. "I don't believe that could be the
one. It doesn't seem to have had much use."

"And yet it seems to me that ought to be the one," said Inga in a puzzled voice. "From the direction of the sun," she went on, thinking aloud, "this one leads southwest, and Halven, where Martin is, is in that direction. Let's see your compass."

The compass bore out Inga's conclusions. "And yet it seems to me," said Petra thoughtfully, "that that trail ought to show more use."

"Well, you see," explained Inga, "right here we are just looking for a connecting trail. It wouldn't necessarily be much traveled."

"That's right," agreed Petra. "I'll tell you what— this trail is going in the right direction. Let's try it for a ways, and we can tell better. Trails twist so, sometimes. We can take our bearings again, and if it seems we're on the wrong trail, we won't have lost much time, and we'll come back and try the other."

"Here we go, then," said Inga, stopping to jerk an extra knot in the red scarf that bound up her fair hair, as if it would be a great help to have that well-secured. Some kind of help was needed, certainly, for the new trail, though reference to the compass proved it to be going in the right direction, was rough and badly marked and hard to follow. It lay close to the face of the cliff, and the mountain plunged sharply downward. Once or twice Inga peered over, as if she was looking for something, but for the most part Petra kept her face straight ahead, for she was taking no chances.

"Do you know something?" demanded Inga suddenly, after one of these downward glances. "There's another trail about twenty feet below us, and I believe

it's a better one going the same way, and shorter. I
know there's a short cut around here somewhere.
Sometimes it's called 'the lost trail.'"

"O, Inga, let's not look for any short cuts or lost
trails. This trail is bad enough, but at least we're pretty
sure it's going in the right direction!" Petra exclaimed.
But just then her foot slipped on a loose stone, and the
next moment she was sliding down the steep side of
the mountain.

She gave one terrified cry as she plunged over the
edge of the trail, and a hundred thoughts seemed
to flash through her mind at once. Would she dash
straight on down to the rocky valley far below? Who
would carry on her work? No one else knew all the
details. She tried to catch at a twisted, outthrust root,
but only succeeded in bruising her hands. Here was a
bush. Perhaps she could grasp that. But she was going too fast. She made one last despairing attempt to
clutch at a gnarled and twisted tree, and now she came
to an abrupt stop, one arm around the tree, her foot
against a rock.

Inga, her face white and her eyes big with fright,
was scrambling as fast as she could down the steep
way Petra had come. "Oh, thank heaven for that tree!"
she gasped. "And that you were quick enough to grasp
it. Otherwise you'd have gone straight over that edge,
and that's a real precipice!"

Petra managed a very shaky smile as she got back
to her feet. "We got down to the other trail, all right,
Inga, so we may as well go along it. I don't think we
can get back to the other one very well, anyway."

"You're all scratched up and out of breath and everything. Let's keep our eyes open for a spring, and you can wash up and rest a little," suggested Inga.

The girls made their way along slowly and carefully, determined to take no more chances on losing their footing, for indeed the way was rocky and the cliffs here very steep. "This certainly looks like a lost trail to me!" exclaimed Petra, longing for a moment's rest after her terrifying experience. "O Inga! There's a little cave or opening ahead there, and a mountain spring. Let's stop and have a bite to eat."

Thankfully the girls made their way to the shelter, and as they rested and ate Margot's delicious rye bread and *lefse*, and Karen's famous butter and cheese, their courage came back. "Now, after this," ordered Inga sternly, "don't you take your eyes off the trail a minute."

"Don't worry," Petra answered, looking much refreshed as she rose from stooping over the spring for a long drink of cold mountain water. Then Inga heard her draw in her breath sharply, and the next moment she had sprung softly to her feet and was moving cautiously out of sight into the very side of the mountain. Inga rose as quietly and followed her.

Petra crept along, carefully making her way between high loose rocks and the cave wall, and a moment later she whispered excitedly: "Inga! It's one of the caves! There are guns stacked here, and boxes."

Inga, close behind her, saw that they were at the mouth of a wide, dry cave, with light flickering dimly through a small overhead opening. "I'd like to investigate those boxes," Petra whispered; "they might hold ammunition." Then voices on the trail made both girls crouch swiftly into hiding behind the rocks. Someone was coming. "Germans!" breathed Petra, clutching Inga's hand hard. Two rough voices came nearer, and it was plain they were quarreling.

"I told you not to leave this cave," said the first Nazi angrily, as he reached the entrance. "We'll get into bad trouble if you do that again."

"You went out to stretch your legs, and you stayed too long. Why shouldn't I go, too? These caves give me the creeps, and the mountains are worse—so lonely and terrible!"

"Well, we're on guard here, don't forget that. And if old Hartsell should come and find us missing, there'd be plenty of trouble, and he's good on the trails, even if he is lame. Come on now—we've got to get these guns counted and in order, and this ammunition. You know we have to get things in order to be ready for the bigger job."

"These are only old junk—Norwegian stuff," said the other scornfully.

"Maybe they are. But when we start work down in Halven, we'll be working with good German manufactures. Anyway, these guns are better in our hands than theirs."

Halven! Why, that was where Martin's school was! What did the Germans want of that quiet little town in the valley? It didn't even have much of a harbor—not nearly so good a one as Valcos. What could they do there?

But the men were going on talking, and she mustn't lose a word if she could help it. She had to listen intently. This was not the High German she knew.

"They don't love us much, these Norwegians. Ja, it's a good thing we got their guns away from them."

"You needn't think we got them all: They've got some left. And they aren't afraid to use them. I don't like it here—two of us on guard alone."

"Quit crabbing and get busy. We'll get the rest of their guns, and meantime we're supposed to be counting these and the ammunition and get a report to Nagler. Next week we have to be ready to help at Halven."

The girls hardly dared breathe as this conversation went on, but the men were talking too angrily to pay attention to anything else, and, besides that, they were very evidently far from suspecting that anyone was near at that moment. If they would just get at handling and counting the guns, that would make enough noise, especially if they kept on wrangling, to give the girls some opportunity to escape.

It was their only hope, they knew that, and when the men went to the other end of the cave and began sorting out the guns, the girls began inching their way out of the cave, moving with painful slowness, keeping always behind the rocks and close to the cave wall.

They were out of the cave at last, and in the narrow opening. Here they had to go even more carefully, for there were no protecting rocks, but this passage angled away from the main cave, so they were at least out of possible sight of the guards, unless they should make some noise that would warn the men and bring them quickly to investigate. This was the hardest part, and the girls hardly dared breathe as they crept silently along, anxious to hurry and get clear of the cave, yet forced to go slowly so as to be absolutely quiet.

They were clear of the passage at last, and in the shallow entrance cave. It seemed to them they had been hours in making their escape, but the shadows told them it had been only a matter of minutes.

Even when they were on the trail, they went along as silently as possible, crouching a little and keeping close to the rocky wall. They looked with longing eyes at a point some rods ahead where the trail twisted a little. Once there, they would be out of any possible sight of the cave entrance, but they didn't dare hurry. Too swift a step might send a stone rolling down the mountain and attract the attention of the guards.

The going was difficult, and it was impossible to make any speed, but they reached the turn at last, and though they did not dare to speak, they looked at each other with thankful eyes. They could go a little faster now that they did not have to be quite so cautious, but they still moved with extreme care, anxious as they were to get as far as possible away from the cave with all possible speed. If only they could get back onto the higher trail!

"Inga, we ought to get off this trail," Petra whispered at last.

"I know that well enough. But how?"

"Look ahead there. Isn't that an old dry stream channel? Couldn't we reach the other trail by that? There are some overhanging bushes that would help."

"Going on all fours, I think we could," assented Inga, and without more words they began their painful way upward. Even when they were safe again on the higher trail, they scarcely stopped to rest, but hurried onward as fast as they could.

Fortunately, they were over the worst part and could make their way more swiftly and easily now, and when they came at last to another fork in the trail Inga gave a low exclamation of delight: "Here we are, Petra. This is right! We follow this fork, and it will bring us out to the trail that leads over the mountain to Martin."

"And that one is stiff going, but it's through the forest, so there will be plenty of chances for hiding. When we get to that, Inga," said Petra firmly, "I'm going the rest of the way alone, and you are going back to the saeter."

Inga smiled in a knowing way, as if she intended to settle that matter herself, but when they did come out safely to the Halven trail, Petra turned to her friend, took her hand for a moment, and said earnestly: "We haven't any choice, Inga. I'd certainly like to have you along, and I know there's hard climbing ahead, but I won't get lost now, and we just can't take any unnecessary chances. If you were discovered on your own mountain, you could easily make the excuse of looking for lost goats or cattle. But there would be nothing you could say here that would bear looking into. And you know there's so much at stake."

"But you? What about you?" asked Inga anxiously.

"Well, one person would be less easily detected than two and could get out of sight more easily. And my ears are sharp, as you know, and I've got used to using my wits these last weeks. I'll be all right. And, Inga, I've been thinking. If we find that it's too dangerous for Sigurd and Ruggles to come back as they planned, or at least for them to land, I'll send the old signal up to you—the little fire in the cove near Ole's—and you must signal them. If it's impossible for me to get back, and there's danger for them in landing, I'll manage to get that fire lighted in the cove where we smoke fish."

"I'll be watching, but how can we get a signal to the boys? We didn't arrange anything," said Inga, looking far more frightened for her brother's safety than she had at any time for her own.

"See that there are no lights, no smoke of any kind—firelight or candlelight or anything at the saeter that night. That in itself would give them some warning. But then if we could only in some way flash a red light." Her eyes fell on Inga's scarf and she cried, "Oh, I know. Of course. Throw your thin, bright scarf over the lantern and swing it back and forth. But, oh, be awfully sure you aren't seen! And now, thank you, Inga dear, for coming with me. And good-by."

"I only wish I could go with you the rest of the way," said Inga fervently. She gave Petra a farewell hug. "Good-by," she said, "and, oh, I hope you'll get back up the mountain to us!" And though she turned away quickly, and managed a jaunty wave of her hand as she went up the trail, Petra saw that there were tears in her eyes. There was a lump in her throat too. When would she see those good friends on the mountaintop again? Her mind was busy with the doings of the night before and the adventures on the trail that morning.

But now she was nearing her destination, and so far she had thought of no satisfactory way of getting in touch with Martin. One plan after another flashed through her mind, but none of them seemed practical. They were all too daring, too dangerous, and so far she had found that the simplest and most natural means worked best.

The Nazis, she knew, guarded the school closely, for Herr Professor Roland, the headmaster, was a fine old Norwegian patriot, and though they had not been able to find anything incriminating against him so far, they were suspicious of him, especially since one or two of the younger masters had got out of the country. Petra smiled a little grimly as she reflected that she could have told the Nazis more than Herr Roland himself about the escape of those younger masters, for they had left in some of the Valcos boats on one of those midnight trips.

But now she must have some plan of action, and then if that did not work when she got there, she would have to try to think of something else. She could tell by the sun that it was somewhat past noon. The boys, she knew, spent some time in the playground just before their midday meal which came at about two. If only she could attract Martin's attention without showing herself! A girl around the school would be so unusual that she would attract attention at once, and the vague and stupid answers with which she had managed to keep herself out of certain difficulties in the past wouldn't suffice to extricate her if she were discovered here.

That old birdcall! That was just the thing! They had used that often to call to each other in the mountains, and even as a signal in games in times past. It was not so loud as one she could make if she had her whistle with her, but perhaps it would be even better for her present purpose. Martin knew her individual call very well. He would remember that! If only she could make it while the boys were in the playground! Then, if she could attract Martin's attention, give him the message, plan with him some course of action, and get home before suppertime, she might not have an impossible amount of explaining to do. Even if she were questioned, she had Captain Ebert's cheese, safe and sound and smelly in her rucksack. She smiled a little grimly as she reflected that only good Norwegian *gjetöst* would have survived her tumble down the mountainside.

She was going down the trail now and, protected as she was by the forest trees, she slid and scrambled as fast as possible. She must get there, if she could, while there was a chance of Martin's being outdoors.

There! She was almost at the foot of the trail, and the buildings of the school were in sight not far below her. Her heart gave a leap of delight, for the boys were on the playground, and her eyes, searching anxiously, found Martin. She drew a deep breath, and then through the mountain air went ringing a clear and lovely birdcall. She thought Martin wavered just a little in his game, but he went on playing, and once again the call went through the wood.

Martin did not so much as glance around, but he suddenly thrust his arm into the air as if he were shaking his sleeve into place. Petra recognized that as an old signal, often used when silence was necessary. She settled down, greatly relieved, in a large clump of underbrush, and opened her rucksack. Martin would be here, she knew, as soon as he could possibly come. In the meantime, the thought of Captain Ebert's cheese had made her hungry. She would rest a little and eat what was left of the lunch Margot had given her. Then, as soon as she had seen Martin, she would be ready to begin the trip home. As she relaxed under the bush, she realized that she would have to be very careful not to go to sleep, for Martin would watch his chance to come, and she must be alert. After all, she was as well hidden from him in this clump of bushes as she was from unfriendly eyes.

The best chance for him to get away, she estimated, would be directly after lunch. She ate hers slowly, so as to keep herself busy until he came. Once or twice she slipped quietly from her hiding place to reconnoiter, but there was no sign of Martin or anyone else. Undoubtedly they had all gone in to lunch. He would surely find a way to get here soon, she felt sure, but the minutes dragged by, and he did not come.

She had had a long and fatiguing morning, and very little sleep the night before. She must not sleep now, she told herself sternly, but she had hard work to keep her lids from drooping. The forest felt safe and quiet and friendly about her, but she knew well that it was not. She shook herself vigorously. Why didn't

Martin come? Very well, then, she would use the time to make plans, get her thoughts in order, so that she could give him all the news in a few sentences. Her head nodded drowsily, but she prodded herself awake. Once more she crept from her hiding place to look for him. Would it be possible for her to get home by suppertime, even if he came now? Had he tried to come and been discovered and stopped? What if she didn't get home this evening? Was Martin in danger at this very moment? Her thoughts were confused and anxious as she started to creep back to the shelter of the bushes. Oh, why didn't he come!

VIII

Petra Goes Fishing Again

P ETRA SAT UP HASTILY, and her eyes flew open. She was conscious of a strong feeling of guilt, but she didn't know the reason. Then with a rush she realized what she had done. Thoroughly tired out, she had fallen asleep in the forest when she should have been on the alert for the slightest word or sign from her brother. Perhaps he had come and tried to find her and gone away disappointed, and all the work and danger had been in vain. Oh, why hadn't she been able to keep awake!

Then her heart gave a great bound, for she knew now what had roused her. It was Martin's voice close at hand and very low: "Petra!"

She came out of her hiding place so quickly as to startle him, and clasped his hands tight, as they crouched down together in the shelter of the under-brush. "What time is it?" was her somewhat surprising greeting.

"It's just after lunch," he answered, and she realized thankfully that she must have crept back to hiding and dropped into a light sleep only for a few moments, and that even then she had been aware of sounds, for Martin's low call had awakened her. There would still be time for all she had left to do this afternoon!

"Petra! This is terribly dangerous for you," Martin was saying anxiously. "Why did you come? You know how zealously we are being watched now."

"Dangerous for you too," she whispered, "but I had to come." She told the story of the evening at the saeter in a few swift sentences. "And now, Martin, the question is, can you make that map? I can tell you where one cave is, for sure. I'll tell you all about that in a minute. Will that help? Can you have the map ready in less than a week's time? How can I get it? How can we get it to Father?"

"O Petra, those are big questions," answered her brother. "But there can be only one answer to the first of them, anyway. It has got to be, 'Yes.' I think I can make a pretty fair guess at the caves—Thunder Cave is likely to be one, Troll Cave another. I will have to watch my chance carefully to work unobserved. I wish we could get Kurt's map," he said grimly, his dark eyes blazing as he thought of Kurt's treachery. "And some-way I'll get the map to you. Keep your eyes and ears open—you'll do that, I know well enough."

"I wish we could get it to Father ourselves," said Petra. "I don't think it will be safe for Sigurd and Ruggles to land up at the saeter again."

"They may have to take that chance," replied Martin, "unless we can find some other way. But Petra, you must get out of here right now. This is much too dangerous for you."

"Just one more thing, Martin." Her brother's eyes grew wide with anxiety and then relief as she swiftly told him about the cave.

"Petra," he said fervently, "promise me one thing. Don't you *ever* take a chance like that again. Promise."

"I promise! Not till next time!" answered his sister in the old gay, teasing way. But he looked so worried that she added, in the soothing tone that had often amused him in the past, for she was small for her fourteen years: "I didn't know what I was getting into, Martin. And, believe me, we got out as fast as we could. But, Martin, in the cave they spoke of Halven, and of course we had to find out all we could. They talked of the bigger job and Halven. Do you know what they could mean?"

Martin gave a sharp exclamation. "Could it be the new fisheries! I've been a little suspicious of those. They are building new fisheries and warehouses and so forth. Their explanation is simple enough. They need fish—more fish for their occupying troops, and also to ship to Germany. But why such sizable buildings, I wondered. Now I wonder even more."

"Could you find out anything about them?"

"I could surely try. But they're very closely guarded."

"Has a lame man been around here?"

"Yes, with Julius Staeck. They are getting a good many supplies through Kurt's store. Hardware, it's supposed to be." Martin was thinking fast. "Hardware and what else, I wonder!"

"Kurt has been in Valcos lately. It may be I can find out something more."

"Well, we both have plenty of work ahead. I'll manage to get in touch with you soon. Now you must hurry off as fast as you can, Petra. Some of us boys have been helping with the house duties since the Germans have taken most of our servants. I came by way of the sheds and can explain that I had clearing-up duty there, if I am discovered and challenged. I will go back the same way and take in a big armful of wood. There is only one guard at this hour, anyway, but the other will soon be back, and I must get out of the woods here before he comes. If I watch my chance, I can manage. Now how about you?"

"If I am home by suppertime, I think I will be safe from too much questioning," answered Petra. "After all, *gjetöst* is very special, and Captain Ebert loves to eat."

"Go, then, but do be careful." Martin gave her hand a hard squeeze and vanished through the forest.

Petra hardly knew how she made that trip home. She was so tired she just put one foot ahead of the other, and where the going was hardest she slid and scrambled. Fortunately this trail, though steep and difficult, was not a very long one, and it was well before suppertime when she came into the home garden and slipped into the house.

She thought she was unobserved, but Captain Ebert's voice boomed out, and it sounded angry. "Miss Petra! Come in here, please!"

With a sinking heart, Petra went into the study. "You left here yesterday without permission," he accused. "Where have you been? I want the details."

"If you please, Captain," said Petra, gathering her wits as quickly as possible and giving him the vaguely polite smile that she had used so often in the last weeks, "you were not here when my work was finished yesterday. I wanted to go up the mountain a ways and get you some very special kind of cheese," she added proudly, and showed him her package.

All this was strictly true and sounded, indeed, so reasonable that Captain Ebert stroked his chin in puzzlement as he had done more than once since he had been a self-invited guest in the Engeland home. This girl, bright enough in some ways, seemed so stupid in others. He could not make her out. And indeed Petra hoped very much that he would not.

She saw now that he was puzzled, and dropped her eyes demurely as she said in a low voice: "Our supplies are so low it is hard to give you much variety in your meals, and Norway is famous for its *gjetöst*. I thought you might like it." Her heart was beating fast. Would he dismiss her, as he had done sometimes in the past, or would he keep her for further questioning, or at least for further conversation? Nimble as her wits were, and quickened with much use these past weeks, she didn't quite see how she could manage to give a satisfactory explanation in that case, and keep from bringing anyone else into the affair.

"If I might please go and wash—" she said, looking up with a small, half-shy smile—"I managed too to get some fresh butter, and I thought I would try to make that German cake which you spoke of last week, for your supper. I think I got the idea, though I wish I had the recipe," and she frowned in concentration as though she were trying hard to figure out the best procedure for the cake.

Captain Ebert looked at her, his brows knit questioningly, but she seemed so very harmless as she stood there, so willing to do all in her power to make him comfortable, that he said, somewhat gruffly: "Very well, then. But remember to be more careful. Remember you are not to leave here again without permission." And he added, as if he really did have some concern for her welfare, "It might not be safe."

"Thank you, sir," said Petra with a curtsey, and ran up the stairs to her mother's room, almost laughing as she thought how surprised the captain would be if he knew how very true those last words of his had already proved to be.

"O Petra!" Her mother welcomed her with a rush of relief and gladness, "I'm so thankful you're home, dear."

"Yes, Mother, and such news! Father's safe in England and hard at work. And oh, such a story as I have to tell you."

"That's enough for now," said her mother softly. "Petra, let me just think of that for a little. Father safe in England, safe and busy there!" The look of sheer joy in her face told something of the anxiety she had been hiding.

"But, Mother!" exclaimed Petra. "When I came in I could see you were excited about something. Has anything happened?"

"Yes," admitted her mother hesitatingly. "Something surprising, and I think important. But you look completely worn out. We'll draw you a bath now, and then you must sleep. When you wake, we can talk. You have much to tell and so have I. Petra, I think we have a job ahead of us, and a big one."

"If I go to sleep, Mother, there's a little job you'll have to do, I guess—a cake for the captain. You remember I told you about it when he tried to tell me how to make it? I got extra butter from the girls, and it's in the kitchen."

Fru Engeland listened, smiling a little as Petra explained the captain's directions. "I can undertake that," she promised. "I wish all the jobs we have to do were as simple."

The house was very quiet when Petra awakened. It must be early morning, and in the soft light she could see her mother seated near the window, her head bent a little forward, her eyes wide open as she stared down into the street from behind the stiff, clean curtains.

"Mother!" whispered Petra, but her mother only put her finger to her lips and did not move. For a few moments longer she sat there, and when she turned and came over to the bed, Petra could see that her eyes were very sad.

"They have just marched Hjalmar Severson and Johann Gilstad off," she said, shaking her head sorrowfully. "They started day before yesterday, taking men away. There are new fisheries at Halven, and the men are to work there, leaving an extra burden, of course, on the ones who remain here, for as much fish

is required from here as before. A few of them go will-
ingly enough—Hans Torgerson, for one, among the
younger ones," her lip curled scornfully—"and those,
they say, are getting good positions. Others—most of
them—are being forced to go. It will be almost like
a concentration camp. They are not allowed to come
home. Much fish is needed to be sent to Germany and
for the troops here, the Nazis say. They are to work
long hours under guard. Ole Haug told me about
it. He is sure he would have been sent too, if they
hadn't needed him in charge of the fishing here. O
Petra, I think of their families too. How thankful I am
your father is in England! I know England is heavily
bombed and surely far from safe, but at least it is not
occupied by Nazi troops, and I have a feeling, Petra,
it never will be."

She told the short, sorrowful tale in a voice that
shook often with deep feeling. From time to time she
paused to get control of herself. Petra did not interrupt,
but when the story was told she murmured earnestly:
"Oh, I wish we were in England too! It seems to me
I can't bear to stay here, with everything so changed.
But no," she caught herself quickly, "Father's work is
there, but ours is here, for now at least. But you spoke
of work for us to do, Mother."

"Yes, dear. Ole Haug thinks, and so do I, that
the fisheries at Halven are a blind of some sort. Ole
manages to nose around quite a bit, and he believes
that they are to be used for war materials of some
sort, though some fish will doubtless be packed
there too."

"So that's it!" exclaimed Petra. "I knew there was something queer—and Martin said—"

"Martin!" cried her mother. "Have you seen Martin?"

"Yes, and he's going to try to find out about those fisheries, and see if anything can be done."

"Oh, that would be dangerous business—extremely dangerous," said Fru Engeland anxiously.

"I know," agreed Petra. "But wait. I'll just begin at the beginning and tell you all about everything."

Her story was soon told, and Fru Engeland held her close as she whispered, "Petra, Petra, I can't let you run into such danger again."

"That's just what Captain Ebert said," returned Petra, trying to make her mother smile, "and he didn't know the half of it. Did you get his cake made?"

"That I did, and he smacked his lips over it. It was a good thought, Petra. It is very important that we keep the officers here friendly, or at least unsuspicious of us, if we can. They have tightened up discipline around here, especially now that they are sending the men away. And they don't mean to let more boats slip off to England. Undoubtedly that Halven business is of great importance also. And, if I'm not mistaken, I heard Captain Ebert speak of those munition dumps. That ties up with your discovery. He thinks my German is far from adequate," and Fru Engeland smiled, for though she had seen to it that her German sounded scanty and uncertain, she had studied music in Berlin and could speak the language almost as well as the captain himself.

"Oh, but now it's more important than ever for us to get some more boats off. We must get as many men and boys away as we can before it is too late, and perhaps some of those guns can arm the boys who go."

"You're right, but I think we must not even wait for the guns, if we can get more boats through."

"No, that's absolutely true. Tonight we must get some boats off, if we can. And in that way we can get a message to Father," said Petra, jumping up with energy. "O Mother, there's so much to be done, and there's so little time to do it!"

"Now I understand why Kurt has been hanging around Valcos so much." Fru Engeland's face was stern as she spoke. "He knows the available men. He is telling the Nazis where to look for help. He knows the ones friendly to the Nazi cause." Her voice fairly dripped with scorn. "I'm afraid he knows which are the loyal Norwegians too."

Petra's mind was working fast. "And, Mother, we must pretend to be friendly to Kurt. We aren't supposed to know what a false friend he is. Perhaps in that way we can even manage to get the map Father wants." She drew in her breath sharply as a new idea came to her. "Mother, while he is still around Valcos, and before he has any possible chance to suspect anything of us, we must invite him here to supper. Tonight we must do it. Right away!"

"I don't know what Captain Ebert would say to that," said her mother, hesitatingly.

"Why, he couldn't object. Kurt is supposed to be a citizen in good standing, and a friend of ours. Of course Kurt would jump at the chance to dine with the officers. And really I think Captain Ebert would welcome it. They must have much to discuss, and few opportunities for long talks. They would probably laugh behind our backs to think of the chance we are giving them."

"But what would we gain, dear? I can hardly bear to have him in this house where he has so often been received in the past as a friend."

"O Mother, don't you see? That will give me a chance to go over to his rooms and try to find that map."

"O Petra, I don't see how I can let you do that! And, anyway, why are you dressing so fast? What are you planning now?"

"I want to get down to Ole Haug's. I want to tell him that if he can get some of the men down to the mouth of the fjord, to the warehouse pier, I know Herr Jorgenson will manage to get a couple of boatloads off tonight. I don't think we'd better try to get any more away from Valcos harbor just now. Ole will have to have time to get word to the men, and they'll need some time to get ready."

"That's right. And of course they will have to go by shore, along that path in the woods. They can't take the chance of going down the fjord by boat, especially now that the Nazis are taking men away."

"And I have something else to talk over with Ole. I'll tell you about it when I come back. I've got to hurry now, before anyone stops me for questions. I'll take my little sailboat and do some fishing." She smiled at her mother, for this was almost a code word with them. When Petra went fishing, she was fairly sure to come back with more than fish.

It was still early, but the summer sun was already bright and high, and Ole was in his little garden, feeding his fine flock of pigeons in which he took great pride.

"O Ole," she said, in great relief, "I m so glad you're here. I was afraid you might have slipped away for a morning ride in that fine *Viking* of yours."

"Oh, no, I have the *Viking* anchored safely away where the Nazis are not likely to find it. I hope to put that to good use for Norway. I have a plan in my mind already, but we'll talk of that later. But you are out early, child."

"I had to come early or maybe not at all," said Petra. "They watch us closely, and about the only way I can slip off is to have the excuse of getting something special for the officers' meals."

Ole looked somewhat ruefully at his pigeons. "Then, remember," he said, "if you ever need me, the pigeons can provide a dainty dish for the captain."

Petra laughed. "Knowing how proud you are of your pigeons, I would say that is a real sacrifice you are prepared to make for Norway," she said.

The old fisherman and Petra were friends of long standing, and they trusted each other completely. Petra told her story quickly, and Ole nodded, understanding some of it better than she had.

"So, then, they have been taking all the Norwegian guns they could lay hands on, and ammunition as well, and storing them in our own caves? Well, I like that! Apparently they mean to gather them all together, if they can. At least, they think they can keep them from us, and have a supply to draw on if they wish to. It seems, then, that even though we are through with organized fighting, our Norwegians are doing some sniping at the enemy. That shows our spirit isn't broken, Petra."

"I don't think Norwegian spirit is easy to break, Ole," said Petra, quietly.

"You are right, my girl," agreed the old fisherman. "Now your father thinks those guns will do more good in our hands than theirs. He wants to get them out of those caves. How?"

"Well, I'm not sure, but I've been thinking about it, and I believe this plan would work," said Petra, who had been turning this subject over and over in her mind. "Sigurd is training to be a Commando. So are some of the other boys who went in those two first boatloads from here. Up at the Holm saeter is a pasture that could be used as an airfield—a small one. Planes could land there, and boys who know our mountains could get those guns if they knew where to look. That's why we must find where they are hidden. Then they could take the guns and distribute them where they will do the most good."

Ole looked so doubtful that she hurried on: "I know that's not the most practical plan in the world, and I'm hoping that we can think up a better one that will work more easily. But I don't see any other way now, and certainly, whatever we do, we must try to have accurate information as to where the guns are hidden. If we can get that information, we can send it to Father with some boatloads of men we should get off tonight or tomorrow. Then maybe Father will have a better plan, or maybe something better will occur to one of us as events go on. One thing is sure—we've got to get those guns away from the Nazis!"

Ole looked at her and nodded. "You have a head, my little Petra, like a tack, even if it is covered with yellow curls. I remember your father and I often laughed and teased your mother about your name, for it seems she wanted you named for your grandfather, Peter, and that means rock. We thought Rose or Felicia or some such pretty and gentle name would suit you better. But now it seems you are well named. Your grandfather would be proud of you today. You think fast and well, and carry through as he did. Now how do you plan to get the information? And had you thought how we might get the men off?"

Quickly Petra outlined her plan. Could Ole get word to Herr Jorgenson and to the men? She would get the map from Kurt's quarters, if she could. Otherwise, they could at least send word to Father of the one cave she and Inga had discovered, and of the others that Martin had mentioned. They could not wait for Martin's map, now that the Nazis had begun rounding up the men and sending them off to Halven. "It will be dangerous for Sigurd and Ruggles to come back and land at the saeter," she said, looking worried. "At first I thought they shouldn't take the risk—"

"And you? This isn't exactly a summer picnic you're planning," said Ole quizzically. "Yes, I can take care of my part all right. We had better tell all the men, when they set out, of the caves we know about, so whatever happens, there is a good chance of that much word, at least, getting through. One must stay behind to take the map, if you can get it. It must be someone who can catch up with the others in time for a midnight sailing."

"Simon Norby?" suggested Petra, for it seemed to her that the young schoolmaster, quick of wit and swift at walking and climbing, would be the man.

"He's your man," agreed Ole. "I will explain to him. Where shall he wait?"

"In the cove between our house and Bjorges', where Kurt is staying," said Petra, who had planned that out on her way to Ole's. "O Ole," she said fervently, "I wish we had some kind of sending station; there are so many messages, and all so secret and so important."

"You seem to be a pretty good sending station yourself," said Ole, pulling down his mouth in a dry smile, "and much safer than a radio. You go home now, and I'll be the sending station for a while. I'll get the word around and things lined up, don't you worry."

As Petra had anticipated, Kurt was so delighted as to be almost smug at the invitation to dine with the officers, and Captain Ebert, though he showed no great enthusiasm, and indeed looked slightly contemptuous, yet raised no objection. "He is an old friend," Fru Engeland explained, somewhat apologetically, "and we should like to invite him here while he is in town."

"Perhaps you and your daughter will give us some music after supper," suggested Captain Ebert.

"We should be glad to," agreed his hostess, "but Petra's long trip for the cheese and butter has tired her somewhat—"

"She can rest today," said the captain brusquely, and Fru Engeland realized that this was an order and that Petra must manage to be back in time to play her violin for them. She dreaded breaking this news, but Petra said quickly: "Why, that's fine, Mother. Don't you see? If I'm supposed to be resting in preparation for the music, it will give me an excuse to be away at suppertime. I'll get back in time for the music, all right."

Fru Engeland found that evening's supper very difficult to sit through. She had engaged to keep the men as long as possible at table so as to give Petra all the time she could for that difficult business of securing a copy of Kurt's map. But as the minutes dragged by, she was finding it harder and harder to make conversation. Where was Petra now? Had she been discovered? Oh, why had she ever let her go? Quick-witted as Petra was proving to be, this was too dangerous. If she failed in any of it, the whole scheme would fall through. Fru Engeland could hardly bring herself to think of it, but there was no doubt what failure might mean. Her life would be in danger. Oh, surely by now she had had time enough to accomplish her mission! Why didn't she come?

Then Fru Engeland sprang to her feet, for there was a sound of running feet along the pavement, a sudden scream, and then a sharp, "But I live here!"

That was Petra! Fru Engeland fairly flew out into the hall, followed by the officers and Kurt. There in the doorway stood Petra, her face so white that the red streak across her cheek stood out like a brand. And on either side of her, holding her tightly by the arm, stood a Nazi soldier.

IX

A Dangerous Errand

WHEN FRU ENGELAND and the Nazi officers and Kurt went into the dining room that
evening, Petra, in her long blue cape and hood, was
poised ready to leave the house, for she knew she would
need every possible moment if she were to accomplish
her task and be back to help her mother to furnish
music for the men's after supper entertainment.

First she went through the pockets of the light
summer topcoat Kurt had worn. She hardly expected
to find anything there, for he would not be carrying
a map around in any such careless fashion, unless, by
the best of good luck, he had brought it along to show
Captain Ebert. But no, she found nothing. Wait a
minute, though. Here were his keys. They would be
a great help, and she set off quickly, not by the main
road, but by a path that ran along the inner edge of
the forest.

It was deep twilight in the woods, but she hurried along as fast as she could, for the Bjorges' house,
where Kurt was staying now, lay at the other end of
the village and she had so little time. If only she could

count on the Bjorges for help, that would be quite another matter. But Kurt would certainly not select loyal
Norwegians for landlords, and indeed Ole had told
her that Herr Bjorge and his son Nels had both gone
to Halven, and he had heard they were to have good
positions there as foremen in the new fisheries. That
spoke for itself. Those good positions were reserved
for friends of the Nazis. But at least those two would
be out of the way. Now, what if Fru Bjorge and her
sister were at home, as they were likely to be? Petra
knew that they would probably be working or sitting
in their flower garden, and there was an entrance on
the other side of the house, facing the fjord. She must
circle around and gain that entrance, hoping that if
the doors were locked, one of Kurt's keys would fit.

As she neared the house, she peered out from the
shelter of the wood. At least, there were no lights,
and she hoped that meant no one was at home, though
she knew she could not count on it. She wondered
how she could gain the house without being seen, and
then remembered thankfully that the Bjorges had a
patch of hay for their cow. The hay had not yet been
cut, and if she could reach it, she could crouch down
in its shelter and have a good chance of arriving unseen at the side of the house facing the fjord.

Very quietly Petra made her way to the hay patch,
keeping as much as possible in the shelter of bushes,
and, crouching down, took a careful look about her.
Yes, Fru Bjorge and her sister were in the garden.
They were having their supper, and Petra hoped they
would linger over it. They were portly ladies who

looked as though they liked to take plenty of time over their meals, but her heart beat fast as she stole to the side door and fitted one key after another into the lock. Yes, this one worked. She turned the key, and it seemed to her that her heart was fairly bursting as she stepped into the hall, and closed the door.

Now, which room was Kurt's? Probably this one, looking out over the fjord. It would be convenient for watching what went on, for sending messages of his own, and for getting quickly to his own boat. But the door was locked, and none of the keys fitted. Here, then, what of this door across the hall? Yes, the key worked, and as she opened the door and looked into the room she recognized a hat and a leather jacket she had seen Kurt wearing earlier that day.

Now, to work! Her heart was thumping so that she could scarcely breathe, but for the first time she was glad of the long, light summer evening. It would have been out of the question to turn on a light. But she didn't need it, and she worked with a precision that would have surprised the efficient Captain Ebert, convinced as he was that Petra was not very bright.

One drawer, two drawers, three! How many would she have to go through? And all articles must be put back carefully, each in the place she had found it. That slowed her progress a great deal. Now, she had gone all through the desk, and there was nothing.

But how about the bureau? She remembered that Grandmother Engeland used to be in despair about Kurt's bureau. He put anything and everything there. Yes, this top drawer was what Grandmother would have called a mess! Quickly Petra went through it. Nothing there for her, but she went straight on to the next, and now she drew a swift breath of joy. This must be it, this long, thin envelope! At the very bottom of the middle drawer, under a great heap of odds and ends! He had thought it securely hidden here, no doubt, in the most unlikely event that anyone should look for it. And she had looked for it and found it!

She was trembling with excitement and dread. If only she dared take it and run to some safe hiding place! But that would never do. What if it should be missed, and she were discovered with it on the way home? Even if it were not missed until later, it would warn the Nazis that the Norwegians knew their plans and even the details. No, her work was not over yet. She must make a careful tracing, conceal it as well as she could in her dress, and leave the original map where she found it.

There were two sheets. That was queer. She didn't understand either of them, but that didn't matter now. Her business was to copy them, not to read them. She laid her plain sheets, her tracing paper, and the maps, on the dresser top and worked with quick, deft fingers, careful to leave no impression on the map itself.

The Bjorge's were taking a good long time at their dinner. But why shouldn't they? They had nothing to fear from the Nazis, and they were set far enough from neighbors to fear nothing from them either.

There, she had finished, and she took a quick look about the room to be sure she had left nothing upset, nothing suspicious. Then, quick as a wink, she went lightly out the door, locked it, was down the hall and out the side entrance. It was then she caught sight of Fru Bjorge rising heavily from the little supper table in the garden. Her broad back was toward Petra, and before the lady could turn, Petra had slipped down the bank out of sight.

Not a moment too soon, either, for Fru Bjorge had turned and was looking intently out at the fjord, and Petra heard her say in a puzzled voice: "Did you hear a noise, sister? I had better go and investigate." And she walked toward the house.

But Petra was safe down the fjord path now. If she could get to Simon with the map, she could draw a good, deep breath again. The cove was not far, and Simon was waiting. Swiftly Petra thrust the documents into his hand, and without a word each turned and went his way. Long afterward Simon told Petra that was one of the hardest things he ever did, for she looked so white and spent that he longed to see her to safety. But that was impossible, and as Petra looked back once, she saw him going swiftly on his way, crouching along the bank. Now he had reached cover. He would make it all right, she felt sure, for he was fleet and sure of foot and quick-witted.

Petra continued her way out of sight along the fjord until she was well back into the village. She wished heartily that she could continue that way, but a deep and steep cove lay between her and home, and she had to come out into the streets of the town.

She was hurrying now, for it was well past curfew, and she certainly did not care to be caught at this point.

If she could just get home without being discovered, everything would be all right. Then not only would tonight's mission be a success, but no suspicion would rest on her in case of future necessary adventures.

She was turning the corner that led to their street when she heard a shout, "Halt there!" and her heart seemed to turn completely over as she heard the heavy footsteps of booted soldiers, for she had suddenly remembered that in her haste to get to Simon and get him off without discovery, she had given him the maps only, and had not taken time to hide the telltale tracing papers with the maps etched upon them. They were tucked away in her pocket. Besides, there were Kurt's keys, where they would be sure to be discovered if she were searched.

She must get away from the soldiers. She mustn't be caught now. Hastily she dodged around the wrong corner, hoping that if they had recognized her they would continue running in the direction of her house, and that she might shake them off, at least until she had time to hide the tracing papers and those dreadful keys in some place where they would not speedily be found. But the hope was forlorn.

"Halt there, you!" came the sharp order again.

Perhaps it would be best to make for home, Petra thought. It might be that she could manage some explanation to Captain Ebert, who thought she was stupid anyway. Perhaps she could throw the soldiers off her trail if she darted under the garden hedge.

But they had caught up with her now. One of them seized her roughly by the arm. "What are you doing out at this hour? Where do you live?" He demanded, and when she did not immediately answer, the other struck her a sharp blow across the face.

"Maybe that will teach you to obey orders," he shouted angrily, and seized her other arm. "Now maybe you'll tell us where you were going so fast."

Thoroughly outraged by the blow, smarting from the pain, and terrified, she managed to jerk out, "Home! I live here! In the big white house!"

Even as they were marching her up the steps, she was trying to make some plan. She had been in danger so many times in the past few weeks that she had become adept at plan-making. Usually the simple ones worked best. But her mind was going round and round now, and she could think of nothing. She felt as stupid as Captain Ebert often thought she actually was. Her thoughts were whirling and it seemed impossible to get hold of them. What of the rest of the plan? Was this the end then? Who would get the word to the Holm saeter? What would she say when they found the map and the keys? Who would be the go-between for Martin and Sigurd? What would Mother think?

They were on the threshold now. Her mother and the men were rushing into the hall. Never in all her life had she seen her mother look so frightened, so heartbroken, and yet so angry.

Petra could think of only one thing. This was the time, of all times, to be half stupid, good-natured, vague, to act as if she could trust Captain Ebert to protect her. He was staring at her now, looking angrily from her to the soldiers, and she sent him an appealing glance.

"I wanted to get a little fresh air," she murmured in a bewildered tone. "My head was aching. I wanted to be ready to play for you."

"Well, that was not such a serious offense, it seems," said the captain harshly to the soldiers. "Surely not enough so that she should be struck, as she was, I see. I doubt that she will get away from you now. She doesn't look very dangerous. You needn't hold her so tight," he added dryly.

The soldiers looked a little foolish as they released their hold. "Curfew is long past," one of them mumbled. "She was walking fast along the sidewalk near the fjord. We called to her but she didn't stop, and when we followed and called again, she began to run in the opposite direction. When we overtook her, she wouldn't answer questions, so—well, our orders—"

"Never mind about that now," barked the captain, and Fru Engeland realized wonderingly that he was taking sides with them against the soldiers. She saw that Petra realized it too, for color began to come back faintly to her white cheeks, and some of the fear was leaving her eyes.

"I was—I was out for a bit of fresh air," Petra said haltingly, her eyes wandering in bewildered fashion about the room. "My head felt tired and queer and I knew you wanted some music. I was trying to clear it up a little. I was frightened when they called, and ran—and when they struck me, I screamed. I was frightened."

Kurt Nagler was looking at her in real alarm. He remembered Petra as a bright and very merry little girl. Could it be that all this trouble had affected her mind? He knew well enough that there were plenty of cases where that had happened. For one terrible moment a rush of guilt swept over him. After all, these people had been kind to him.

"Petra!" he said, in the tone he had often used to her in childhood. "Don't be frightened. You are safe now."

Kurt's words steadied her far more than he had expected them to. Indeed, such a torrent of anger swept through her as he spoke that, to her mother's relief, she straightened her shoulders, pushed back her hood, smoothed her hair, and said with dignity, "If I may be excused, I will put myself in better order, and will then be ready to play for you."

"You may go," said Captain Ebert, and added reproachfully: "You see now what I meant when I warned you to be careful. I said it was not safe for you to be out alone."

Petra nodded humbly. "I meant to go for a little walk," she repeated vaguely.

"Yes, yes, I know. Go then. We are almost ready for the music."

Petra, as she went upstairs, thought never had home looked so welcome.

"You may go now," said Captain Ebert sharply, turning to the soldiers.

He was finding the whole affair most distasteful. He knew well enough that the soldiers must maintain order, yet he was angry that this harmless girl, who did so much for his comfort, should have put herself in the way of discipline. She must be more careful. It would not do for him to protect her again.

He stepped closer to the soldiers and tapped his head significantly as he said, "Not too bright. But good at the violin and does her best to keep us taken care of. She is harmless enough. Give her a little lee-way, if necessary. We will try to see that she does not break curfew again."

Petra's first move was to hide the sheets of tracing paper. Each had a map on its face, and if Simon's were lost, they could use these, and might indeed be very glad to have them. Her grandfather had had a little desk made for her, with a real secret drawer. It had always been a source of great delight to her, but so far it had held nothing more important than a few special notes and mementos. Now she was thankful to have so good a place to hide her papers. When those were tucked safely away, she quickly put on her prettiest dress, brushed and arranged her hair. She must get the keys back into Kurt's topcoat pocket somehow. Just how she was going to manage that she had no idea, for the hall was in full view of the living room where the guests were sitting. She must make an opportu-nity somehow, and though there would probably be no time for private conversation with her mother, she was sure of her co-operation.

How could she play tonight, wondering about those keys, wondering how the men were faring, won-dering how soon Simon would reach Jorgensons', how soon the boats could put off? They must wait until the sun made its short journey below the horizon. There would be little enough time this short summer night.

Suddenly she remembered Fru Bjorge's garden, and an idea came to her. Her mother's garden was equally fine. She ran downstairs now, and joined her mother at the music cabinets where she was making some selections for the evening's playing. "Get the men out into the garden for a moment," she managed to whisper, as they discussed the music.

Her mother barely nodded, but a few moments later she said, "O Captain, I want you all to see my roses in this white summer evening light we have here. Let us do that while Petra gets out her rack and tunes her violin."

The men agreed readily to so pleasant a sugges-tion, and, when they were safe in the garden, Petra in a flash had the keys safely back in Kurt's pocket. She was busy tuning her violin when they returned.

As she played the wild Norwegian music, her ex-citement rose and communicated itself to her mother and to her audience as well, for now she was having a reaction of relief and exultation at the success of her danger-filled evening.

"I have heard you play many times," said Kurt, "but never better than tonight."

"Do you perhaps play some German music?" asked the captain.

"Yes, but let us save that for another evening. We must brush up on it in order to do it justice," replied Fru Engeland, for she felt it was high time Petra was in bed, and moreover she was exceedingly anxious to hear the whole story.

The evening was over at last, and safe in their room, Petra was unfolding her tale.

"Well done, my Petra!" said her mother, giving her a fervent hug. So that was the reason for the visit to the garden. I knew there was something. But are you sure you left no evidence of your visit to Kurt's room?" she asked, anxiously.

"I'm sure I didn't. I just escaped having Fru Bjorge see me, but she is nearsighted, you know, and I was over the edge of that bank in a hurry. She would have come and shouted, I think, if she had been at all suspicious. That's what I was afraid of. I wanted to get Simon off, safe and sound. O Mother, just think—the message I was so worried about is on its way to Father. And, besides, we have a copy of Kurt's map here in case we need it. If the boys come back, it will be because they think the chance is well worth taking. But I must try to get word to Martin that he doesn't need to take time to make that map. There is plenty of other work he'll want to be doing now. He is right there in Halven, where those make-believe fisheries are."

"This time I think we will wait for Martin to come to us," said her mother firmly. "You have done too much already, taken too many risks. You must take care for a little while, or they will begin to suspect you, no matter how stupid you act. Better just stay home for a few days, and make some cakes and some music for the captain. It is well we were in his good graces tonight. That is part of our job." Fru Engeland smiled, but her eyes were proud as they rested on her daughter. "Martin will come, never fear. There's work ahead for all of us. We must be ready," she said.

Petra knew well enough that her mother was right, but it irked her to be kept so close at home when there was so much that needed to be done. Thursday passed, Friday and Saturday. Why didn't Martin come? Could it be that he had been put to forced labor in the Halven fisheries? What could he be doing? When would they get word?

X

Martin Goes Investigating

M ARTIN OPENED HIS EYES with a start, and sat up in bed, his heart pounding. He glanced sharply around, puzzled at the strange surroundings. Instead of his own comfortably furnished room in Halven School, he saw bare rafters overhead with skis and fishing poles stored across them, and old trunks and broken furniture stacked in the corners. The luminous light of the Norwegian summer night showed these things plainly, and as sleep cleared away, he remembered that he had asked Herr Roland for permission to sleep that night in the high, unused tower room of the dormitory.

It was an odd request, but the Herr Professor knew Martin well, and he merely said: "You have a good reason, I am sure. Do you wish to tell it?"

Martin hesitated, for in the few weeks of the Nazi occupation of his country he had learned through grievous experiences that not every fellow countryman could be trusted. There was Hans Torgerson, for instance, his old friend and playmate, who had turned, as everyone knew, to the Nazis. Indeed, Hans was said to hold a good position right now in the Halven fisheries. But Martin knew there could be no question of Herr Roland's loyalty. A finer old patriot could not be found in all of Norway. So much had been proved already. And the wise counsel of the old schoolmaster would be most useful and welcome.

"It's about the new fisheries, sir," he replied. "I think there's more there than just fisheries. I'm sure they are a blind for something much more important."

He had expected his teacher to look surprised and perhaps skeptical, but the old gentleman said quietly: "I agree with you, Martin. But just what do you expect to find out in the tower room?"

"Well, sir, I have a feeling that the Nazis are bringing equipment in here at night. The fisheries are too far from the village for anyone to see them then, and they probably know that the school sleeping rooms are on the other side of the building."

Herr Roland nodded. "The loads they bring in in the daytime are harmless enough, it is true, and they unpack them quite freely in plain sight—fishing equipment and fish-packing equipment of all kinds. It may be that they are bringing in other things at night, though why they would bother to take the precaution is a question. They have little reason to care what we suspect or think."

"We may not be quite so helpless as they seem to feel," said Martin proudly, "or so dumb." Then he added, "Oh, I've heard them calling us 'dumb Norwegians,' but I believe we can do quite a little to stop them, or at least to delay them."

"Go, then, sleep in the tower room," said the professor. "But don't fire on any of them," he added dryly, and they both smiled, for it was well known that though the Nazis thought they had confiscated all Norwegian guns, many remained carefully hidden in Norwegian hands.

Now Martin, wide-awake, was listening intently, sure that some unusual noise had roused him. Perhaps it was just the heavy summer rain, sounding very loud on the tower roof. But no, at regular intervals, above the sound of the rain, came the "chug-chug" familiar to every fjord boy—the engines of the sturdy fjord freighters.

In one leap Martin was out of bed and kneeling before the small window of the tower room. Sheets of rain were falling, but through them he could see a procession of small fjord boats drawing up to the pier of the new fisheries.

If only the rain would stop! It did that often enough, as suddenly as it began. And Martin, shivering in the chill damp of the long unused room, knelt there doggedly, determined not to move until he saw what those boats were going to unload. They had just arrived—he was in time to see that. Undoubtedly they were only waiting for the rain to stop before they unloaded their cargo.

Martin glanced at his watch—two o'clock. He had been right in his guess. It was plain that the boats had arrived in the hope of unloading at night and getting off again before the town was awake.

There, the rain was subsiding a little—another moment or two and it would be over. Now it was clearing, and Martin held his breath with excitement, for activity was starting on the new pier. Men poured out of the fisheries, others appeared on the decks, and the unloading equipment was quickly set up. Cargo was coming up from the hold, and Martin's eyes were wide open, his heart pounding, his mouth dry.

Those great boxes and crates! Fish-packing materials never came in anything like that. What in the world could they hold? Martin had never seen anything to compare with them. Guards were posted at all entrances, and up and down the pier; men were hustling the big packing cases into the warehouses. It was all done with a swiftness, a precision, that showed careful planning behind it.

For almost two hours the activity continued, and Martin did not stir from his post until the last boat chugged off down the fjord.

How many nights had this gone on, he wondered. How many of those huge cases were housed in the new fisheries? What could they contain? That they held something very dangerous to the Norwegians he was sure. He must find out, if he could, what it was. He must find out much more about this whole affair.

The first step was to get permission to be absent from school that day—to be free to prowl around wherever he thought he might get any information. Perhaps he could get Herr Roland to entrust him with a few errands that would take him to various shops and offices in the little town. Per Olson, the gossipy baker, might have some news. Or Gunnuf Hovde, the quiet but wide-awake butcher, might know something that would throw some light on the matter. He could stop for a haircut. Anton Lund, the barber, usually had his eyes open and knew what was going on. And it might be well worth his while to stop at Kurt Nagler's hardware store. He had always enjoyed going there, and he could hardly believe the discovery his sister Petra had made, that Kurt was a Nazi spy. Kurt was out of town now, still busy with the lame man probably.

If only he knew some loyal Valcos man who could help him to get the information he needed about the fisheries—someone employed there. But the loyal Norwegians were given only menial work, and would have no opportunity of finding out about anything. His heart was heavy as he thought of Hans Torgerson. It didn't seem possible to him that his old friend could be a traitor to Norway. If only he and Hans could work together on this. But that, of course, was out of the question.

As Martin had expected, Herr Roland readily gave the permission needed. "So you were right about their bringing in material!" he exclaimed, when the story was told. "And now what is your plan?" As Martin unfolded it, the professor nodded agreement.

"Martin, are you planning to go to the fisheries?" he asked, looking straight at the boy. "That would be very dangerous; surely you realize that. It would probably be impossible in any event," he added thoughtfully, "for it is fenced off and marked ferociously with 'No trespassing' and 'Verboten' signs."

"I know that," agreed Martin. "Yet I must get on those grounds if it is at all possible. If only I could find some legitimate reason for being there"—he broke off, trying to think the thing through. "You see, it's information of that kind I want to send to Father in England. If we can get definite information to him, he may be able to use it to very good purpose."

"That is true," replied Herr Roland. "Go then. But try to use the utmost caution."

On the streets of the little village of Halven, Martin was thankful that he had definite errands, for twice he was stopped by the soldiers.

"What is your business, young fellow?" they demanded harshly, and Martin was very glad he could give a direct reply.

But though he went into more than one shop and made guarded inquiries, he found no one who could give him any information that was useful. Kurt's hardware store was almost his last hope.

But when he started to go in there, he was halted sharply. "I need a hammer," he said urgently, for he had a feeling that activity was going on in there, and it seemed unbearable to be stopped.

But the soldiers only laughed. "We can do all the knocking around that's needed here," said one of the soldiers, and the others roared their appreciation of his humor.

"Very good! Very good! Yes, we can hammer out about everything we want. Go on about your business, boy. The hardware store is too busy to sell hammers to Norwegians."

The mocking laughter of the soldiers was hard enough to bear, but when Hans Torgerson passed by, glanced from Martin to the soldiers, and joined in the laughter, that was far harder. Then, as Hans went on his way, he gave one more glance over his shoulder, a glance that made Martin catch his breath sharply and turn down a side street. For something in that quick look made Martin feel that Hans had something to say to him. But as he turned the corner, he saw that Hans was walking straight on, with never a backward look. He had been wrong then; that glance meant nothing, after all.

He had exhausted every possibility—Per Olson knew nothing, or was afraid to speak. Gunnuf Hovde shook his head when Martin asked, with meaning in his voice, if the new fisheries had had any effect on his business. Even his friend the barber could give him no information. In Kurt's store he might have used his eyes and ears to good purpose, but he was not allowed to enter. He had found a last ray of hope in Hans's look, but now that had failed. He had hoped above all to find some reasonable errand to take him to the fisheries. He knew well enough, that, carefully guarded as it was, he could never hope to enter without some very good talking point. Somehow he had hoped that Hans might help him, after all. But that had fallen through too. He would have to try to manage in some way to get to the fisheries at night before the boats came again. But he realized that that was a forlorn hope indeed, and his heart was heavy as he walked down a little-used path to the fjord. He wanted to be alone for a little while before he went back to the school with only failure to report.

And then he thought he heard his name called, very low. He shook himself impatiently. What was the matter with him, anyway? Was he getting light-headed from too much planning and too little sleep? But the low call came again, "Martin!"

He walked more slowly and glanced cautiously about. On his right was a small, deserted boathouse, and now he knew that the voice came from there. Someone might be watching. This might even be a trap. Casually he stopped and looked the little boat-house over, and then, as if he might want to see what its condition might be, he opened the little door, care-ful to keep his hand on the knob.

"Come in, Martin," said the guarded voice. "It's me, Hans. You needn't be afraid. I know what you're thinking, but it's not so. Come in, and quick."

"Hans!" gasped Martin. "What are you doing here?"

"I watched to see which way you were going, and then hurried ahead to waylay you. Oh, I know you all think I've gone over to the Nazis, but I haven't. I found out I could learn some things we needed to know that way. I learned that much from Lieutenant von Berg, who's quartered at your father's house. I know every-one trusts you. When I saw you there at Kurt's store, I thought you were trying to find out things, maybe were even working with someone, and I knew I could help."

All this sounded very welcome to Martin, but he was in no hurry to commit himself. Certainly he had no intention of telling about Herr Roland, about Sigurd Holm and Petra and the others. All this could well be a trap.

But Hans was hurrying on. "I see you don't trust me, and I don't blame you. But I'll tell you, Martin, if you're wondering about those new fisheries—and that is what I think you are doing—they're just a blind. We Norwegians don't work much at night, though something goes on there, I'm sure, certain nights at least. But tonight I'm on duty from four until midnight. If you'll come down about eleven, the guards are pretty sleepy then. I'll arrange to have some kind of treat for them, and maybe they'll want a nap. Sometimes they do that. They don't think we're very dangerous. And, besides, I've made it my business to get in well with them. They won't bother us. Come to the little east door and just whistle like this—very softly. I'll be there."

"But it's all fenced in," said Martin. "How could I get to the east door?"

"The fencing isn't finished. You know the big rocks up toward the school. They have to fence between those, and they haven't been able to get all the blasting done yet for the posts. You can get in there. Now you go. Walk on toward the fjord as you were doing, and I'll slip out of here. We mustn't be seen together. Be there at eleven. Don't oversleep or forget!"

"Don't worry! I'll be there!" answered Martin, but his thoughts were in a turmoil as he walked on down the path.

Could he trust Hans or was this just a trick? Should he tell Herr Roland and ask his advice? No. The old professor, stanch patriot as he was, would hardly feel he could give permission for one of his boys to run into what looked like certain danger. For Martin realized clearly that if he went he would be taking a grave risk. And yet if he could get any real information about the fisheries, it would be invaluable.

He made a brief report to Herr Roland, tried to eat some supper, and went to his room. His good judgment told him he should sleep the early part of the evening and set the alarm clock for ten. He did try to follow this sensible plan, but he was far too excited to go to sleep. Was he about to find out something of great importance, or was he about to step into a trap that might land him in a concentration camp?

His mind flew to another project, one that he knew he could profitably discuss later with Herr Roland. It was the discovery Petra had made, that Norwegian guns had been confiscated and hidden in caves in the mountains. Many times that week he had thought of his promise to make a map of the caves where he thought some of the guns might be. He had given it a great deal of earnest attention, and had begun work on the map, for he was sure he knew at least some of the caves that would be used. He wanted it to be his very best effort, since it was to go to Father. The week had gone by with many demands on his time, and he had had little opportunity to work on it. He realized suddenly that it was tomorrow night that Sigurd and Ruggles were coming again. Tomorrow night they would try to fly over from England and land again at the Holm saeter. He must finish that map now, and find a way to get it to the boys. But suppose they did find the guns? What would they do with them? That was a question he would like to discuss with Herr Roland. Father might have a plan ready, of course, but how pleased he would be if they could handle it from here!

He worked with absorbed interest on the map, and by the time it was finished it was time for him to start. He slipped down the back stairway, with the anxious hope that no one would stop him for explanations. He had made up his mind it was well worth while to take the risk, and he didn't mean to be stopped. He went down into the cellar, and out one of the windows, and from there, very carefully, to the rocks Hans had indicated.

He wished fervently that the night were darker, but summer nights so near the midnight sun were never very dark. Now at eleven a pearly twilight softened even the rawness of the new buildings. Crouching here among the rocks, he mapped his way. There was little shelter to be found between here and that east door, for the ground had been carefully cleared. But there was some rock left from the blasting, and one or two piles of material covered with tarpaulin. Martin crept very carefully from one of those spots to the next, hiding between moves, and reconnoitering.

Making his way over this forbidden ground was nervous business, but worst of all was the uncertainty as to what he would find at the end of his pilgrimage, even if he were successful. His heart was pounding so that it almost choked him as he neared the fishery.

What lay behind that east door? He made his way to it and silently turned the knob, fearing that a guard would grasp his arm as he entered.

But no gruff and guttural voice challenged him. Instead he heard Hans say, in a low voice of intense relief: "You made it, Martin! Good for you! Now we've got to act fast. The guards are catching forty winks—" and he jerked his head toward an adjoining room from which came the comfortable sound of snoring. "I've seen to it that they've done this before, and I've always called them in time, and taken over their duties, which aren't very heavy. Only tonight I borrowed the keys too. Now, let's hurry. The new guards will be here before twelve, and you have to get out of here before that, and these fellows have to be awake and alert."

Together the boys went silently down the corridors. Martin knew well what a fish-packing plant looked like, and at first this seemed ordinary enough, only larger than any he had seen.

But then Hans unlocked a door. "You'd better go on alone from here, Martin. This is strictly *verboten*," he said, in a voice tense with excitement, "even to the most trusted Norwegian workers, if there are any such. I'll stand guard. I can make some excuse. You couldn't. I'll try to warn you so you can at least hide if there's danger. Go fast. And watch. They may be working in the other wing."

Swiftly and silently Martin went down the corridor, glad now that it was not completely dark. He knew he needed to make good use of his eyes and that this was a rare opportunity. A door opened, and a voice said sharply, "Who is there?"

Hardly daring to breathe, Martin managed to slip in between some high-piled boxes, thankful for their great size. "Who's there?" came the voice again, and a second voice said dryly, "You dunderhead, you're always thinking you hear things! If the cat walks by, you think we're in danger of being blown up or something. It's my opinion you don't want to help with the cleaning up. Come on, now, we'll catch it if we don't have everything in order when Captain Ebert comes to look things over."

Captain Ebert! Then he was connected in some way with these fisheries! So all these projects were really hooked up together. The footsteps had died away now, and Martin peered out. A faint crack of light outlined a door at the end of the long corridor. Activity was going on there, all right, and Martin wished with all his heart that he could know what went on. But there, he knew, he could not enter. Well, then, he would find out all he could right here. This was a warehouse, of course, well filled with enormous boxes and with smaller ones as well. An unfinished door at right angles to this corridor stood partly open, and Martin longed to creep down that aisle between the boxes and peer around that half-open door. He tried to decide whether the risk was greater than the chance of finding anything worthwhile, but even while he was weighing the question, his feet were slipping silently along beside the boxes. He moved with extreme care, for he knew men were working not far off. He had almost reached the door when he heard steps once more. This time the sound died away in the other direction, and he immediately resumed his careful inching along.

He reached the door at last and peered through the opening. Then he caught his breath, for his quick eyes had detected something he had surely not expected to find. Stowed away in a corner were barrels marked "Dynamite." Martin gave a surreptitious glance around. Suppose a guard should appear. But he had to find out if those labels spoke the truth. Fairly holding his breath, he crept across the little room and looked in. Yes, there was dynamite, no doubt of that! Did the Nazis intend to use this? Was it just left over in building? Maybe the Norwegians themselves could find a use for it if they could just get hold of it!

As fast as he dared, Martin made his way back to the main corridor. He was none too soon, for hardly had he reached it when he heard the low "Ssss!" the signal he and Hans had agreed upon. "Quick now! It's time! You get back to the rocks as fast as you can! Wait for me there," whispered Hans, as Martin reached him.

In a twinkling Martin was out of the east door and creeping back up the hill. His heart was in his mouth, for now there were plenty of sounds around the fisheries. But there was little activity on this side which faced the school. The Nazis preferred to keep most of the business on the sheltered fjord side.

With a feeling of intense relief, Martin crouched down among the rocks to wait for Hans. He waited for what seemed to him a very long time. It would be too bad if his old friend had got caught in his first chance to help. But no, again he heard that low, "Martin." Hans had circled around and come from the other direction. "What did you find out, if anything?" he whispered eagerly.

"They are working in the other wing, but I suppose you knew that."

Hans nodded. "Yes, I thought so. I wish we knew what they are working on. It's important and dangerous, I'm sure of that. They work there till midnight many nights, and sometimes till four or five o'clock."

"And, Hans, there's dynamite there. Did you know that!"

"I suspected it. But I didn't know where it was. Maybe that's information that will be valuable. Have you any idea—"He checked himself. "No, I mustn't even know what you have in mind. The less I know the better. I have an idea you can make use of what you found out tonight. Now I must go."

"O Hans, can't you come with me? Do you have to go back into that danger spot?"

"It's the best way I can help," said Hans quietly. "The hardest is having folks think I'm a traitor to Norway."

"I'll tell them the truth," burst out Martin, but Hans shook his head.

"Not yet. The news might leak out in some way, and then my usefulness would be over. We'll have to wait. You go on about what you have to do now, and I'll do the same."

"Good-by! Good luck! We'll get together again, and soon, I hope," said Martin.

His mind was seething with ideas as he hastened back to the school. What were they making down there in the plant—something so important they worked all day and more than half the night. What were they going to do with that dynamite?

XI

A Meeting on the Mountaintop

B Y SUNDAY EVENING Petra had almost given up hope of Martin's coming, and she lay awake a long time that night. "Sigurd and Ruggles will come, and Martin will not be on hand," she thought. "I must manage to get there myself. No use to try to fool ourselves any longer. Something must have happened to Martin. Otherwise he would surely be here now."

At last a reluctant drowsiness overtook her, and she was almost asleep when she sat straight up in bed, clutching the covers about her, and her mother, with a frightened start, sat up too, for they knew that someone was in the room, someone who was being very, very quiet. Petra's thoughts flew to the secret drawer in her desk. Had someone found out about those tracings? Was he looking for them here? Did he suspect her? What if that someone should know about such hiding places? What if he should open that secret drawer?

Then both of them almost cried aloud in sheer relief and joy, for Martin's voice came through the soft semidarkness: "Mother! Petra! Quiet now. There's so much to tell and so little time to tell it."

"But, Martin, how and when did you get here?" asked his mother. "We can talk pretty freely tonight. Captain Ebert and the others are away—I don't know for how long, of course. No one is here now but Otto, and you can hear him sleeping."

They all laughed as they listened to Otto's comfortable snores. But Martin kept his voice low as he went on: "You can't be too sure who's around. I just got here and climbed the tree and into your window, but I must get back before things are stirring. They're watching us pretty closely at school. It's almost the end of the term, and they seem to think that means we'll make a dash for freedom. Maybe they're right," he added grimly.

"You came over that terrible trail at night?" demanded Petra.

"Oh, that wasn't much," said Martin with a smile. "If that was the most dangerous business I'd been doing these last few days, I wouldn't think I'd been very daring. These summer nights aren't too dark, even in the forest. Now listen. I've brought the map I made, but I'm not satisfied with it at all—"

"Petra got Kurt's map," his mother broke in, her voice proud and eager, and the main points of the story were soon told.

"Petra, that's wonderful!" said her brother huskily, and under cover of the darkness gave her hand a quick, hard squeeze. "I never thought you could—well, never mind that now. I'm about through being surprised at you. And, in fact, this gives me good hope that you can help in the job we must do now. I'm the one who told you not to take any more chances, and now I'm asking you to run right straight into danger." He hesitated, as if not sure how to go on, and then said, "I told Herr Professor Roland about the caves and the guns."

"That was a good thing to do, Martin," approved his mother. "There are not many I would care to take into our confidence in this important matter, but there is no question of the Herr Professor. He is loyal, through and through, and wise, and, I believe, shrewd."

"Yes, he's all of that," said Martin eagerly, greatly relieved at this reception of his news, for he had not been sure they would approve of sharing such a secret even with the Herr Professor. "I was puzzling and puzzling about those guns, wondering how we could make use of Petra's discovery, wondering how we could get them out of those caves before the Germans did—they won't leave them there long—and those caves are not good storage places for guns."

"I thought maybe Sigurd and Ruggles would come back with a plan from Father, if Simon and the others got through. Ole found out they went in some good, fast boats," said Petra. "Sigurd and Ruggles are due Monday night—why this is *now*, the wee, small hours of Monday morning. The boys will be here tonight!" she exclaimed. "What are we to tell them?"

"Even with the best of luck, the second boatloads would hardly be there yet," answered Martin, "and, anyway, I'm certain Father would be pleased and relieved if we could take care of those guns over here, and I'm hoping that is the message we can send back.

They'd rather leave the guns here in Norway, I'm pretty sure, and Herr Roland thinks so too, than take them anywhere else. The Germans won the first round of the war with us, but it's not all over yet—don't you think it. Someday we'll get them out of here, and we're going to need those guns. And we know how to use them. They're Norwegian guns, you know, confiscated from hunters and farmers and everyone."

"What's your plan, Martin?" asked his mother. "For I can see you have one."

"Well, to begin with, we know now those new fisheries aren't just fisheries. I found that out, and Hans Torgerson helped. Oh, yes!" he hastened on, as they interrupted with surprised exclamations, "we all thought he'd gone over to the Nazis, I know. And, believe me, he hated to have us think that. He was doing it to get information, and he's been a big help." He hesitated, wondering if it would worry them too much if he told them of last night's adventure. But they might need to know, especially Petra as she went on with the work that lay ahead. "I got in there last night," he said briefly, "with Hans's help."

"Martin! You didn't!" cried his sister, in excited admiration.

"Martin!" said his mother in a lower tone. "Was it necessary?"

"Well—yes, I thought it was. I knew they were bringing in too many men to work there, and too much material. And I think I made some important discoveries." He sketched his adventures of the previous night and added: "Your officers are connected with it in some way. They are over there now, looking around, and inspecting things."

"So that's where they are!" exclaimed Petra. "We wondered. Now, Martin, what is the plan you and the Herr Professor have about those guns?"

"Well, you know he's always taken us to his summer home up the mountain at Lillegaard for the last week or so of the term. We didn't think they would allow it this year, but they are pretending to be quite friendly now, probably because they don't want to stir up any more trouble for themselves than they have to right now, with this new project in Halven. So when Herr Roland went through the form of asking permission to take us on this short camping trip, we were all surprised when they promptly gave permission."

"They want you out of the way for some reason," said Petra thoughtfully.

"Maybe. But I think they're just trying to show that they aren't so bad as some folks think," said Martin. "And I believe they'd like to make a friend of the Herr Professor, if they could. Of course they can't, but they don't know that. They do know that he's influential, and that though his school is small it's one of the best in Norway."

"Maybe you're right," said Petra, somewhat doubtfully. "Well, go on."

"Today—Monday—is when we go. Well, here's the big thing! Up at Lillegaard is a great, dry storeroom built into the mountainside. Herr Roland says it's been there as long as any of his family can remember, and long before that. He thinks it may have been a hiding place in the old days when robbers and brigands roved these mountains. It is so cunningly made that you can't possibly find the entrance unless you know where it is, and even then it's not easy. He has never spoken of it, and it's as safe a hiding place as there is in all of Norway."

"In your week up there at Lillegaard, you boys are going to try to get the guns and hide them there?" Petra said in a thrilled whisper.

"That's right; and oh, how I wish that map was here instead of on its way to England!"

"Oh, but I have the copy on the tracing paper!" cried Petra. "We didn't quite finish our story, we were so anxious to hear yours."

Quickly she got out the paper, and Martin studied it eagerly. "This is it! This is it! I see now. Yes, yes, they chose the caves well. And best of all they are not too hard to reach from Lillegaard. No, I won't have to take this map. I have it all in my mind. I'm going to leave this with you."

"But my part in all this—what is my part?" demanded Petra.

Martin hesitated, as if he found it very hard to go on. "Do you think you could get that map up to the Holm saeter by tonight? I'd ten times rather do it myself, but I don't dare take the chance of being missed from school. The permission might be taken back, and the whole plan wrecked."

"Why, yes, I can do that. Of course I can," agreed Petra eagerly.

"I hated it enough to ask you to do it when I thought you would just be taking this poor excuse of a map I made. I hit some of the right places at that," he added, with some pride, as he spread out his map. "But now let's get it out of sight. Put it with the others." He went on slowly, "That would have been dangerous enough if you were caught. But now I have to ask you to take the good map—Kurt's map. Petra, you simply don't dare be caught with that in your possession, especially after what happened the other night!"

"O Martin, I can't let her go!" exclaimed Fru Engeland. "I will go myself."

"O Mother, no," said Petra, giving her mother a jerky hug. "You're not so good a mountain climber as I am, and that's not saying too much. And I've been over the trail so recently, I know the dangerous spots and the hiding places. And if you were gone from home, they would really raise a hue and cry, and everything might be discovered. No, I'm the one for the job," she managed to speak lightly. "You know I'm always wandering off and finding some nice tidbit to add variety to the officers' meals. I can do it again. I'll start right away. Funny, isn't it, how some people like to go strolling around at night? I've often heard that when things get tense enough, it drives some people to sleepwalking."

"I might tell that to Captain Ebert if he returns and misses you," said her mother, trying to take up Petra's light tone.

"O Mother," answered Petra, excited and eager now that she could get to work again. "Maybe that's an idea. But perhaps, with them gone, we can get by for once without questioning. If you'll wait a few minutes, Martin, we can go part way together."

"There is one other thing I must do," said Martin. "Get word to Ole Haug. We may need help from the men down here in collecting those guns from the caves and getting them to Lillegaard. We must arrange a meeting place and a signal."

"And, Petra, we must hide these maps somewhere where they wouldn't find them easily in case you were—overtaken. While you dress I will loosen the lining of your mountain boot and slip them in there," said Fru Engeland, sounding much calmer than she felt. "We'll hurry now. If you can both be well on your way before morning, so much the better."

Her throat ached as she watched the two steal quietly through the garden and vanish into the woods. What would happen before she saw them again? Her own task of staying at home and trying to keep all smooth and serene was not the easiest of the three.

"Good-by, Petra. Good luck," said her brother fervently, as they came to the parting of their ways. "You know the trail pretty well now, don't you?"

"Oh, yes, that doesn't worry me this time. But, Martin, I was wondering how we are to get word to each other. You must know what word the boys bring. They must know about your plan for the guns—how well it is going, and all that."

"I've been thinking of that too. We go to Lillegaard today, and we intend to work fast—the faster the better, of course. Tonight or tomorrow night we should begin without fail." He thought hard for a moment. "I should talk to them first, tell them what we're doing. And I should know what word they bring from Father. If it's at all possible, I will get up to the saeter myself tonight. We can't count on it, but I'll try. If that's impossible, tell them we'll try to get at least one more boatload of fishermen off with messages. Something better may develop, and I know now we can depend on you, Petra, to act according to the developments. Sigurd knows how to use his wits too. I'll be up there if there is a chance in a hundred. You can depend upon that."

Petra nodded. She knew it would be dangerous, but both of them were used to that now. There was no safe way to do these things that had to be done.

"Look out for the lame man," warned Martin. "He was down in Halven yesterday. I'm thankful for that, anyway, but you can't count on his staying there. He certainly does get around."

Martin looked so anxious that his sister said reassuringly: "Yes, but they do seem to be so busy at Halven they aren't paying quite so much attention to other things for the moment. This is really a good time for us to be getting these things done."

"I wish we could find out exactly what they are doing there," said Martin. "It's important, we know that, and they're certainly concentrating on it. Something has got to be done about those fisheries. But we've got to get the job of the guns out of the way first."

"That's right," nodded his sister, and started off up the trail, while he took the path to Ole Haug's. When her trail angled, she turned to wave at him. He was standing in the middle of the path, looking after her so anxiously that she gave him a very bright smile and a vigorous wave of her hand.

And indeed she felt lighter-hearted than she had felt for days. It would go hard with her, she knew well, if they took her and found the maps in her boot. But the mountains had provided hiding for her before, and a help to them all. They did not seem so fearsome to her now. And it was a satisfaction to be doing something again. With so much to be accomplished, the inactivity had been hardest of all to stand. Tonight the boys would come again, and then they would all know how things stood and what action they could take next. They might even know if that last boatload of men got through, and how their plans were working out with Father's, though Martin thought that most unlikely.

A bluebird flew across her path. It lighted in a tree almost over her head and burst into song, and Petra found the friendly little act very encouraging. She kept alert to every sound, but perhaps all the Nazis really were down in Halven, for there seemed to be no one on the trail but herself. She hoped with all her heart that they would keep themselves busy in Halven all week, or at least until the plane had made its visit and the guns were safely stored in Herr Roland's dry mountain storehouse.

She climbed the last high bank and ran up the path to the saeter cabin. But no one answered her greeting. No one was there, and for a moment she felt almost numb with fear. Had the Nazis come up here and taken the girls away? She hurried out to the milking yard and her spirits rose with a bound, for there were the three sisters, busy at the morning's milking. She was so relieved that she felt suddenly very gay, and leaned over the fence, smiling broadly but not saying a word.

It was Inga who saw her first, and she jumped up so fast that she almost upset her milk pail. "Petra! Petra! Oh, we were so afraid you couldn't get here. This is the last day, you know. Tonight they come again."

"I know that very well, and I was worried too, but here I am, and with such a map!"

The milking was finished in short order, and soon the girls were at breakfast, while Petra told them of all that had happened during the past week, and they listened wide-eyed, interrupting often with questions and exclamations.

"I'd just like to know," said Margot, when the story was finished, "what they are up to at Halven."

"Martin says it's something terribly important, but they haven't been able to find out exactly what, so far," answered Petra.

"I've been wondering," ventured Karen, a little timidly, "what if the boys can't come tonight? How will we get all this word to your father?"

"They'll come," said Petra confidently. "By the way, have you seen anything more of the lame man?"

"No one's been around. I believe," said Inga, "they were trying to hunt out safe places for those guns. It looks as if they think that part of the job is taken care of, and now they are leaving some guards around, like the ones we saw, but the most important men are down at Halven, and a few at Valcos."

"Maybe we think that because we hope it," said Karen, smiling a little.

"Sounds reasonable though," said Petra, and in spite of herself she yawned, for now that she had accomplished her journey safely, she began to feel relaxed and drowsy.

"Look here now," said Margot briskly, "you didn't sleep much last night, that's sure, and you've got to have your wits about you tonight. No telling what's ahead. So I'm going to put you to bed while the rest of us get our jobs out of the way."

"I'll help with the jobs," protested Petra, but the sight of Margot shaking out the big feather beds and putting them into clean linen cases was very pleasant.

"You get ready for bed," ordered Margot, spreading one fluffy feather bed on the couch in the corner and holding the other in readiness for a cover. "Quick now."

No sooner had Margot tucked her in than Petra was sound asleep, for she was thoroughly tired out. Hours later she awoke, much refreshed, to find Inga looking somewhat anxiously down at her.

"Oh, I thought you'd never wake up," said Inga, greatly relieved to see that Petra's eyes were open at last. "But Margot wouldn't let me wake you—said you probably hadn't slept much for nights, and needed all you could get after all your excitement and danger.

Wouldn't you like some supper now? You've not much more than time to get dressed. And the boys should be here within an hour or two."

"Supper! Why, have I slept all day? I'll be ready in five minutes," said Petra. "I want to get those maps out too. You girls haven't even seen them yet."

As they sat at supper, Petra spread out the maps. "There were two sheets, and I copied them both. Martin spotted this one right away, and said it was of the caves. The boys will want to see that one, of course, but I don't know what this other one is. Maybe nothing important, but here it is, anyway. Oh, I hope the boys will come!" she exclaimed, for now that the moment was almost here, for the first time she had a little doubt.

It might be absolutely impossible for them to come. None of the girls spoke of this, but all of them knew that the plane might have been shot down before ever it got back to England.

"There it is!" cried Petra suddenly, for her quick ears had caught the distant sound of a humming motor.

All of them jumped up with joyful cries, and a moment later they were running out with their lanterns to the pasture, to guide the boys to a safe landing. Petra had remembered to slip the maps quickly into the secret recess under the window before she left the cabin, for she recalled the lame man's visit the week before, and she had learned to take no unnecessary chances.

Inga stood guard as before at the window while the boys talked and examined the maps. They had not yet seen the ones Petra had sent to England. Those boats, they said, had not arrived before they took off, though they were sure they had caught sight of them almost in port.

Suddenly Ruggles gave a sharp exclamation. Sigurd, whose familiarity with English had increased daily, listened intently, his face white with excitement, and Petra, who understood every word he said, was fairly holding her breath as she listened.

"Ruggles thinks this second map is the plan of an assembly plant," Sigurd translated to his sisters.

"Oh!" cried Petra eagerly. "Maybe it's the Halven fisheries. Maybe that is just what Martin needs to find out."

"If only he were here!" exclaimed Sigurd. "We could—"

Sigurd never finished that speech, for a sound broke into the night that fairly stunned that little group around the table. It was the starting of an airplane engine.

"Someone knows we're here. Someone had an airplane parked near by," jerked out Sigurd. He glanced swiftly from the secret recess to Margot. "Is the trap door in there clear?" he asked.

Margot nodded. "Of course. We've got it all ready. We knew it might be needed any time," she answered as swiftly. "We can hide you."

"No, that isn't it!" exclaimed Ruggles. "It's our plane, Sig! Someone knew we were here, all right, but that's not a strange plane! That's our plane! But someone else is flying it!"

XII

A Night on the Mountain

THE LITTLE GROUP in the saeter cabin rushed to the window, Sigurd in the lead. They were just in time to see their plane rise from the pasture landing field and fly out over the valley.

"There it goes!" exclaimed Sigurd, and they looked at each other with despair in their eyes. "Now, how do we get back to England with this report?"

"We'll have to figure out some way," said Ruggles. "It's evident they're trying to keep us from getting back to England in time for our information to do any good. And Captain Engeland is so anxious to get it."

Sigurd started to rush to the door. "We've got to find out who took our plane!" he cried. "It might help us in getting it back."

But Ruggles, who had been on more than one Commando raid, held him back. "Not yet! We don't want to get in their shooting range. This may just be a trick. They certainly want to keep us from getting messages back to England—or probably from doing anything else. They'd like to find out who we are all right, and I surely wish we knew who they are. Might help us to do something about it."

"I think I know!" exclaimed Petra. "They'd recognize me fast enough if I went out now, but as soon as they're out of sight, I'll go and investigate."

"Not alone," protested Sigurd. "We'll wait till we can all go."

As soon as the plane had disappeared over the mountain, they sped toward the pasture. "Yes, see!" cried Petra triumphantly, "here where the ground is soft! Always there is one footprint much deeper than the others. It's the lame man, and one other."

"The lame man who almost caught the boys last week!" gasped Inga. "Tonight he was quicker."

"I'm afraid of him," said Karen shivering. "He tries to make his talk sound pleasant, but his eyes aren't pleasant. And he's too clever."

"Oh, I don't know," returned Margot scornfully. "Petra outwitted him on the trail. And she and Inga found some of the guns he thought he had so safely hidden."

"He's clever, all right," said Ruggles, as they walked back to the cabin, "if he's the one I think he is. And he's a dangerous man. I know of other jobs he's done. It's a high mark for Petra that she's outwitted him. He's clever, but he has a stupid streak too, because he's too sure of his own cleverness."

"I hope he doesn't suspect we have those maps," said Karen soberly.

"And now we know how important they are!" burst out Sigurd. "O Rug, we've just got to find a way to get back to England with them!"

They were back in the cabin now, spreading out the maps again. "Petra took a dangerous chance to get these," said Ruggles. "We have to find some way to make use of them, even if we can't get them to England."

"Every cave where the guns are hidden is shown here," said Sigurd eagerly.

"And this other one!" cried Ruggles in sudden excitement. "I have it now! Look, Sig—"

"Listen! Someone's coming!" breathed Petra warningly.

A sharp knock at the door made Karen sweep the maps off the table into hiding, while Margot whispered, almost soundlessly: "You boys must hide. Come!"

But it was Martin's voice that cried, "Hey, let me in there! Quick!"

Petra flung the door open with the joyous cry, "Martin! You did get here! I didn't think you could!" And now the tense silence in the cabin was broken with shouts of welcome, with rapid questions and swift explanations.

"I wasn't alone on the trail. I knew that. That's why I was in such a hurry for you to let me in. It must have been those fellows who took your plane. I only hope they all got away in it. We don't want them around tonight!"

Martin had had a long climb, and the other boys had come from far. All of them were very hungry. Margot and Karen brought out rye bread and cheese and plenty of milk.

"Eat now," said Margot, for she had a sensible theory that food was important ammunition. "You'll need it."

"That's right," agreed Martin, "we've got a big night ahead."

"Even bigger than you think, maybe," said Ruggles. "Do you know what's on this second map?" He could talk easily to Martin, who spoke and understood English well.

"I didn't realize there was a second map that amounted to anything," replied Martin.

"It doesn't amount to anything more than a plan of an assembly plant," said Ruggles, his voice low with excitement. "And it looks to me like an airplane assembly plant! Is there anything around here—"

Martin struck the table with sudden comprehension. "The Halven plant!" he exclaimed. "So that's what it is—an airplane assembly plant. Why, of course! That explains the big boxes they were bringing in. We knew it was something important, but we thought it might be guns they were assembling there. Yet the boxes were too big, we thought. We were trying to find out—"

Now Ruggles was speaking again, in short, jerky sentences, and those who understood English were listening intently. Now and then one would give a short, purposeful nod, or put in a word. Martin translated briefly: "That plant is too dangerous. They think it is a safe place for them, up the coast here and right on the fjord."

"And Halven has flat ground for small landing fields," added Sigurd.

"It may be they intend to take the guns away in those planes," suggested Petra.

"Righto! and they have plenty of other uses for those small planes. They could assemble enough there to patrol all the coast of Norway and more besides. Put a big crimp in our raids," said Ruggles. "We've got to get back to England with all this news, and get there fast." He frowned as he tried to think of a way.

"We might get a boat out tomorrow night," Martin suggested doubtfully.

"Boats are so slow—" objected Ruggles.

Petra clapped her hands in sudden excitement as an idea came to her. "They've been working down there at the Halven plant hard and fast," she cried. "If they're really assembling small planes there, couldn't it be possible that at least one would be ready? Could it be that you boys could find a plane there to take you back to England? Fair exchange for the one they took?" she added, half laughing, for the plan seemed so audacious she was afraid the boys would laugh at her, and she thought she might as well laugh first. She remembered too late that Martin often made fun of her ideas about machinery. Probably it took months to assemble a plane. What did she know about it?

But to her relief and astonishment, the boys were looking at her in frank admiration. "I think you've got something there," said Martin. "They have been working hard and fast, as you say."

"And they'd be anxious to get one ready for testing," agreed Ruggles. "It certainly is worth looking into." He was silent for a moment, and his face was grave as he said, "One thing is certain. The Halven plant must not be left there."

"Do you mean you must come back and bomb it?" asked Petra unsteadily.

"That would be one way," returned Ruggles. "But with our plane gone, we might not be able to get back here soon enough—they can do a great deal of harm in a very short time if they get those planes going." He hesitated and then asked, "Would they have used dynamite in making the foundations?"

"It's rocky there," Sigurd answered quickly. "They'd have to do quite a lot of blasting."

Martin's face was very grave, but his eyes were bright with excitement as he said: "I know they used dynamite. They intend to use more. There's quite a lot down there. I know where it is. I found that out."

No one spoke for a few moments, though all of them realized well enough what the others were thinking, and the faces around the table looked tense and white, even in the yellow candlelight.

Martin broke the silence at last, and his voice, harsh at first, grew more natural as he went on: "Our first job is to get the guns. We have that all planned, and we know pretty well how to proceed. We must try to get them all to safety."

"You're right, Martin! That's our first consideration. But do we have the man power?" asked Ruggles. "Your father only expected us to bring the information of where the guns are hidden."

"That's what we'll send him," returned Martin, smiling a little. "Only it won't be information of where the Nazis have the guns hidden. We'll send

word to Father that we Norwegians have got hold of
them again and have them in safe hiding. That job at
least has got to be done tonight." He talked very fast
in Norwegian, translating for Ruggles whenever necessary. "The fact that your plane was taken shows that
the Nazis suspect we're up to something." He turned
to the maps again. "This shows some of the guns in
Jotun Cave, Troll Cave, Thunder Cave—we can get
to those without too much trouble. The others too we
know how to reach."

"Fine! Fine! Couldn't be better," cried Sigurd, and
added, with a little smile, "Your father said it wouldn't
surprise him if you folks here had some plan worked
out. This is going to please him a lot."

"But the man power?" persisted Ruggles. "And
where do we hide all those guns even if we can collect
them?"

"In a great, dry cave at Lillegaard," said Martin,
and quickly explained the plan. "There is plenty of
room there," he finished, "and a secret passage, need-
ing some repair, connects it with the cellars of the
main buildings."

"That's just the place!" exclaimed Sigurd. "There
the guns will be handy to give to the men and boys
who sail out on the fishing boats to England, or escape
in any other way. And some of them can be kept for
future use here in Norway. But, as Ruggles says, what
about the man power? How do we get all those guns
to Lillegaard?"

"The older boys from the school will help,"
responded Martin, "and a good group of men from
Valcos. The girls here are to set a signal fire under the

cliff as soon as we leave. Ole Haug has notified the men, and they will be ready to set off for Lillegaard as soon as they see the signal fire. They'll make good time. They're used to these mountains. I arranged that with him this morning."

"Righto!" exclaimed Ruggles. "Sounds to me like good planning. Sig, maybe someone did us a favor when he took our plane. I'd like to help with this business. It's going to take good, fast work."

"It would be great to have you," said Martin, his face full of relief. "You've had experience with this sort of thing that none of the rest of us have had. You could take charge."

"If you say so," agreed Ruggles, "with your help and Sig's. And right now, while the lame man is out of the way is the time to get at it. Before they have time to nose out your plan, Martin."

"Could it be," suggested Karen, the most cautious of the group, "that he suspects something of the kind and intends to circle the mountain with that plane, watching?

"Smart girl," agreed Ruggles, as Martin quickly translated. "We'll have to be on the lookout for just that. But even this near the midnight sun there's a sort of darkness and a period of twilight in your mountains for a time."

"And that time will soon be here, said Sigurd. "Let's get going."

"I'm coming too," announced Petra.

"No," objected her brother, "carrying guns is no work for a girl," and the other boys nodded in very definite agreement.

"Oh, yes, I'm coming," said Petra firmly. "Maybe I can't carry guns, but I've got sharp ears and eyes, and they may come in handy. And you'll need a guard at the storeroom. They may be watching Lillegaard."

"I'm coming too," said Inga. "I can help guard, and both of us can help stow the guns away."

"So could I," offered Karen, and shy and timid as she was, they knew this offer meant real heroism.

Sigurd patted her shoulder and said gently: "Someone has to stay here, and that's not the easiest job either. But suppose anyone came to ask questions, and no one was here."

"Yes, and someone has to light the signal fire for Ole," said Martin. "He'll be watching for it, and he'll have the men at Lillegaard about the time we get there."

"Karen and I will tend to all that," promised Margot, but her eyes were wistful as she watched the others go off down the path. She would have liked well to be one of the number.

Martin was talking fast as they went down the trail, outlining the details of the night's work as he and Herr Roland had planned it. Ruggles interrupted now and then with a word of approval or a practical suggestion that greatly improved and simplified the plan.

"Ruggles, that lame man surely did us a favor when he stole your plane," said Martin. "You're worth a dozen inexperienced men, and more. You've told us how to manage some of the points that were bothering me most—how to slip up on the guards without being seen, how to get them out of our way for a while, how to get the best results with the fewest men." He was silent for a moment and then burst out, "Would I like to be a Commando!"

"Don't worry. That will come," replied Ruggles quietly. "In the meantime, you're doing a man-size job here, Martin."

"Plane coming toward us!" cried Petra, and the five hid quickly in the shelter of some pines, for the Norwegian night was not yet very dark, and figures on the trail could be detected from an overhead plane. "Isn't that your plane?"

"That's it, all right!" exclaimed Ruggles, examining it with his glasses. "They are searching for us, no doubt of that." Two or three times the plane circled over and then flew off. "Good thing your mountains here are so high they can't fly very low. And it's getting darker now in these valleys."

"Good thing there are other valleys they have to investigate," said Martin.

"Yes, and we'll soon be safe from sight. We're nearly to the forest," added Sigurd.

Not until the plane was well out of sight did they venture from their hiding place. Then they walked slowly, with few words, until they had reached the shelter of the forest. From there on, the going was speedy, for the trail was well hidden.

Herr Professor looked surprised when he saw five returning when he had expected one. He welcomed the boys heartily, for he knew they would be of great help, but he looked somewhat questioningly at the girls.

"They wanted to come—help guard and so on, sir," explained Martin, looking slightly embarrassed.

"And they have already been most useful—spotting a plane that might have spotted us," explained Ruggles.

Herr Roland smiled. "I think from what I have heard that Petra has a right to help just about wherever she chooses," he said. "Inga too helped discover the cave, I hear. It is dangerous—" he sighed—"but that does not stop them, I see that. Go and wake the older boys, Martin. I have explained to them about the night's work."

Rousing the boys was easy, for once. All were eager to be off. Ruggles' clear, crisp orders, translated by Martin, put everyone into action.

Hardly had the boys disappeared up the trail when Ole Haug appeared from the other direction with a group of men. Once again the plan was swiftly outlined, the orders given, and the men, grim-faced and silent, set off.

Petra's face must have shown how she longed to go with them, for Herr Roland patted her shoulder and said, "I am very glad to have such competent helpers. We must get the door open to the cave. We must watch with the greatest care that no one steals quietly up here, that no one sees us. We must plan for the quick disposal of the guns."

The girls were so curious to see the great storeroom in the mountainside that they followed Herr Roland eagerly. Straight into the woods he led them. There was no path, but he seemed to know exactly where to go. And presently they stopped in front of a sheer, rocky cliff, with moss growing over the stones. Could it be that he thought they were in need of a rest before a further climb? Petra was about to reassure him when her eyes opened wide with a start, for in the dim twilight of the woods, she saw a narrow, rocky door swing open a little, and as Herr Roland stepped over the threshold, they followed and found themselves in a great, dry room, where even a whisper was swallowed up in the dark silence.

"Martin said the opening was cunningly contrived," Petra gasped. "Why, they'll never find this!"

"You're right about that. And yet it is accessible enough so that we can supply guns to the men who leave from these parts, and have some left for ourselves when we need them. From here we can distribute them where needed. Now we had better wait right here. We must take no chances of being seen if that plane should come over."

"Troll Cave isn't so far away. The boys should be back from there before too long," said Inga, and though she knew it was too soon to expect them, she began already to listen, for Sigurd was in charge of that group, and she was anxious. "Shall I go out to the trail and watch and guide them here?" she asked restlessly.

"A good plan," Herr Roland replied. "And Petra shall fill in the details I have not yet heard."

Petra, thankful for the opportunity to take counsel with someone as wise as the old schoolmaster, poured out the whole story. "If Father were here, he would know just what to do," she said wistfully, "but he is doing important work in England. Both Ruggles and

Sigurd say he is invaluable. But we all know you are so wise, and you knew just what to do about the guns. Now something must be done to get rid of the assembly plant there at Halven, and Sigurd and Ruggles must manage somehow to get back to England. I don't know just what we can do about the plant. Maybe it's a job for someone else. But I know Ruggles thinks something should be done without any delay. But I thought we might—we just might get a plane down there for the boys."

"You have posed some big problems, Petra," said Herr Roland, very thoughtfully. "You must let me turn them over in my mind."

"O Herr Roland," burst out Petra, "the boys, I'm afraid, have a plan in mind, and it's so dangerous, I can hardly bear to think of it. We can't let them do it."

The cave was very dark and the silence was thick about them. It was so long before the old schoolmaster spoke that Petra wondered, if, after all, the problems were too big for them to solve.

At last he said, very slowly: "I too see that there is a way—a dangerous way. It may be the same one of which you are thinking. It would take courage, which is one thing, and daring, which is quite another, and dynamite, which is still a third. But I think I know where all three can be found."

But before he had time to say more there was the sound of hurried feet in the woods, and a moment later Sigurd's voice came, low and urgently: "Where is that opening? We must get these guns under cover quickly. A plane has been circling over."

XIII

THREE BOYS GO TO HALVEN

E VEN IN THE MOUNTAIN FOREST, the Norwegian summer night was not entirely dark. The men and boys of Valcos and Halven knew these mountains well, and the caves and trails were familiar from days when they had been used for hunting and fishing trips and much mountain climbing.

Sigurd's group took Troll Cave for their objective, Martin's detachment went to Jotun. The men set off for the Cave of the Winds.

There was little talk, for the orders had been clear and concise, and though the leaders expected no interference on the trail, all knew that silence was necessary. Indeed, no one felt like talking, and hearts were pounding as the little companies walked swiftly and silently on an unaccustomed errand along the familiar trails. What if the guards had been reinforced? What if they overpowered the little parties of inexperienced boys and men?

As Sigurd's group neared Troll Cave, they heard voices. The guards were wide awake. "I'm tired of this stupid job," one was grumbling. "I want to get down to Halven where there's something doing."

"*Ja*, there's nothing to do up here. These dumb Norwegians—"

But that sentence was never finished, for Ruggles knew well how to proceed, and he had given his orders clearly. Sigurd crept softly around the rock into the cave opening, the others followed silently, and before the guards knew what was happening, they were overpowered by the "dumb Norwegians."

"They'll sleep soundly till morning," said Sigurd grimly. "Now for the guns!"

Quickly the first load was parceled out among the carriers, two boys were left to guard the cave, and the others marched swiftly off with the rescued guns.

Down in Lillegaard, Inga crouched beside the trail listening, her heart in her mouth. She had spent plenty of nights on a mountain, but then she was safe in the saeter cabin, or in some jolly camping group. She had never realized that a night alone under the mountain sky could be so full of sounds. There—a twig snapped—they must be coming. But no, she had to settle down again, only to spring to her feet in a few moments at another false alarm. But here they were coming at last. There was no mistake this time. She jumped up in relief and joy, and fairly flew up the trail to meet them.

She led them through the dim, thick woods, straight to a cliff rising sheer out of the forest. Through a nest of boulders they went, but even with the cave door standing slightly ajar, she had trouble to find it, so well was it concealed.

Once through the opening, the boys found themselves in a large dry storeroom built into the side of the mountain. Much as they wanted to gaze about them, they knew they must wait for that until later. Speedily they deposited their guns and left them for the old professor and the girls to stow away, with help from Fru Roland, then went back for another load. As they went on their way, the second group came in.

All of them had been on the lookout for the stolen plane, and everyone was greatly relieved when the new group reported that it had flown away. "It circled over once or twice and had us worried," said Martin. "But fortunately the woods are thick, and they didn't catch sight of us or they never would have flown off."

"They seem to think they've stopped whatever we were planning to do by taking our plane," chuckled Ruggles, and added with sudden grimness, "They are in for quite a surprise."

The boys were scarcely on their way once more when Ole Haug's company of men came in with their larger loads. Through most of the night they worked, with swift, precise action, and when their work was finished, the cave storeroom was well stocked with guns and ammunition.

"Now," said Herr Roland, "you are all to go to the dining room, where Fru Roland and the girls have breakfast ready for you. And you, Martin and Ruggles and Sigurd, stay here. Here is Petra coming with breakfast for us. We still have some matters to discuss."

As Petra entered the storeroom with her tray, Herr Roland was speaking. "We must see that all is in order. And I will show you now how to close the door from within. I will show you too where the underground secret passage comes in. It leads from here to a concealed closet connecting with the main cellar, but I don't know what condition that passage is in. It has not been used for a long, long time."

"That will be something for a few of us older boys to do—clear it out this week?" suggested Martin eagerly.

"A good idea. We will do that," agreed the professor. "But first, boys, while you have been getting the guns, I have been turning over in my mind all we know about Halven, and now I think I have for you another project, and a big one. We will see what our friend Ruggles thinks of it. He, I believe, can take charge of it. From what Petra told me, I believe you had some such idea in mind yourselves, and I have been working out details."

"Here is breakfast," said Petra, hoping she sounded calm enough so that they would not send her away. The plan the boys had thought of but had scarcely mentioned on the mountaintop—that dangerous plan she had dreaded to see them embark upon—that was the one they were going to discuss now. "Please let me stay," she said so earnestly that no one had the heart to refuse.

"Very well. Come and join us," said the professor. "You have earned the right, I think."

The door was closed now, and a lantern lighted the cave dimly. But Petra, sitting quietly and listening, saw that the light in the boys' eyes was very bright as they made rapid plans.

"The Halven fisheries!" exclaimed Martin. "Yes, the sooner we can get those out of the picture, the better."

"Those ought to be polished off tonight," agreed Ruggles emphatically. "Small airplanes assembled here could do a terrific lot of harm to this coast and to our communications with England."

"If only we had our plane to get us back to England, we could come right back with a load of bombs," said Sigurd. "Or with dynamite—" he looked quickly from one to the other.

"There is dynamite enough there," said Herr Roland. "Martin found that out." He paused, and now it was his turn to look from one to the other of the boys.

For a moment no one spoke. Then Ruggles said in a matter-of-fact tone: "You're sure they're not working at this hour? I'd like to see that assembly plant blown sky-high, all right. That's what ought to happen to it, but I surely don't want to do any harm to these brave Norwegians if we can help it."

"Do you understand how to use dynamite, Ruggles? You've used it?"

"Oh, I've used dynamite," cried Martin. "So has Sig. When we built our camp on the mountain, we had to blast out some rock—"

"Yes, but this is in much larger quantities," said the professor.

"I know how to do it, sir," cried Ruggles, his eyes shining with excitement.

Martin looked at his wrist watch. "This is a good time," he said "And the sooner the better. Those guards in the cave are going to come around all right, and they'll spread a warning. What we want to do, we'd better do now."

"What are we waiting for?" asked Ruggles quietly.

"Let's get going!" said Sigurd.

"But, Herr Roland, if we blow up the fisheries, we will blow up the school!" cried Martin. "The village is far enough away to be fairly safe. But the school can't escape!"

"That is a sacrifice we must make, Martin," said the old professor quietly. "We can carry on the school elsewhere—even up here at Lillegaard if necessary."

"I say," said Ruggles, somewhat taken aback, "I don't like to destroy your school. But an airplane plant there could do tremendous mischief."

"It is not the school that concerns me," said the professor, and they could all hear the anxiety in his voice. "It is the safety of you boys. This is dangerous business to send three lads on."

"War is dangerous business, sir," returned Ruggles quietly.

In the dim light of the flickering lantern Petra could see her brother's face. He would go she knew, and in spite of her sick fear, she knew she could not try to keep him back. She saw Martin set his jaw in a line she knew well. "You are not sending us, sir," he said. "We are going of our own accord."

"Even up on the mountain, we all felt that it would have to be done sooner or later," said Sigurd, "and this seems to be the time." He sounded as calm as the others, but all were tense and alert.

"Then you must go quickly," directed Herr Roland. "Before the village is awake, and while only guards are in the plant."

"Come, then," said Ruggles. "Let's get going."

Petra's face was strained and very white, but she managed to whisper, "Good luck!" Then she hurried back to the kitchen to help Fru Roland and Inga.

The road from Lillegaard to Halven was steep and rocky, but it was not long. Most of it lay through the pinewoods, and the boys were able to make good time. As they went swiftly down the trail, Ruggles outlined details of his plan:

"Sig has already had some training, and that's a good thing. Martin's getting his first lesson right now, the hard way. You're not afraid?"

Martin shook his head and set his jaw hard.

"Maybe you are—just a bit," said Ruggles, smiling a little. "So are the rest of us. But we'll do the job just the same."

The little town of Halven was very quiet when they paused at the edge of the wood to reconnoiter. "No houses near the fisheries—they saw to it that it was isolated, thank heaven for that," commented Ruggles, swiftly taking stock of the situation.

"Just the school," said Martin in a low voice.

"Our Herr Roland can hold a good school without those buildings, you know," Sigurd spoke with assurance.

"Now, remember, if there's a plane ready, we take it," whispered Ruggles, winding up his few clear, definite instructions. "Martin sees to the rest. If there's not a plane for us, up goes the plant, anyway, and we make for the woods. Sig and I get the guards out of the way first. The rest is up to Martin. Sure you can do it?"

"I can do it," answered Martin firmly, but his mouth was dry and his heart was pounding as he looked down at the familiar scene. There lay the buildings of the school, with the village in the distance. He was concentrating on the shortest and safest route to take.

"There's a guard," whispered Sigurd. "We've got to be careful."

But Martin had his way planned now. "Come on," he whispered back, as the guard went out of sight around the corner. "Just follow me. We haven't a minute to waste."

Up in the little summer house at Lillegaard, Herr Roland was straining ears and eyes toward the valley when Petra found him. "You!" he exclaimed. "You should be on your way home. The men all left here some time ago."

"All except Ole. He is waiting for me, and we are going a roundabout way and come in where he has a small fishing boat waiting, so that we come from up the fjord toward home, fishing as we go. But O Herr Professor," she said, in great agitation, "I can't leave until we have some word!"

"And Inga, where is she?"

"She is going to stay and help Fru Roland today, and get up the mountain when things have quieted down a bit. I've been working and helping too, but I feel so anxious, I just had to come out and talk to you. Shouldn't the boys be there now? Surely we'd hear the noise if—Has anything gone wrong do you suppose? I've been thinking—I didn't do one thing to try to keep my brother from going into that terrible danger! And even if the other boys get away in a plane, what about Martin? He's to be left here! And even you? They may suspect you both!"

"That is not likely, I think," said Herr Roland, trying to comfort her, though he was as anxious as she was. "Don't blame yourself, child! You couldn't have held Martin back, and you wouldn't want to."

"No, of course not," she admitted, "I know that."

"And if they succeed, not only will the plant be blown up, but, you remember, the school is not far off. It can't escape either. They would not expect us to blow up our own school. No, the dynamite was left there for some purposes of their own. They certainly would never think we could get in, well-guarded as they keep those fisheries. It could look like an English job, of course, or it could look like an accident. They will probably think, 'Those dumb Norwegians!' That is what they think of many of us, you know, and you yourself have proved, Petra, that it is a useful thing."

"If only the boys aren't seen—" Petra began, but the sentence was never finished.

For through the still air came the sound of an explosion, another and another. Then intense silence. Her eyes were anguished as she looked at the professor, and between them was the unspoken question, "What of our boys?"

Then their eyes filled with eager hope, for a welcome sound broke the silence. Across the blue morning sky a plane came flying, a new plane. It soared over Lillegaard and was gone, off toward the sea and England. But something fluttered down on the little lawn, and Petra ran to get a bit of paper weighted by a cartridge.

"It's a note!" she exclaimed, and together they spread it out to read.

"M. safe and on the trail to L. Thank you—you'd make good Commandos—but right now Norway needs you just where you are."

"They know what they are talking about," said Herr Roland thoughtfully. "There's much to do here, and you have shown you can do it, you and Martin, both. And now, Petra, it is high time, and more than time, that you were getting started." He put his hand on her shoulder and added gently, "I know well you would like to be working in England with your father, and the time for that may come later, but right now you would rather stay and do your job here, is it not so?"

Petra's eyes were on the plane, now only a speck in the distant sky. She watched it out of sight, and her eyes were misty as she turned back to the professor. "As Ruggles would say," she answered, smiling a little, "righto!"

XIV

CAPTAIN EBERT INVESTIGATES

M ARTIN STUMBLED into the little clearing at Lillegaard and looked anxiously about him. His immediate concern was to find Herr Roland and give a report on the mission to Halven. He sighed with relief as he saw the professor hurrying across the lawn toward him.

"You did your work well, my boy," said Herr Roland, putting both hands on Martin's shoulders. "We heard the explosion. A little later we saw Sigurd and Ruggles in their plane. They dropped us a note as they flew over, but gave us, of course, no details."

"Yes. Well, the Nazis won't be assembling their little planes at Halven for some time," said Martin grimly. "The village wasn't hurt much, but the school's mostly gone."

"I expected that, of course," returned the professor quietly. "But we can carry on our school right here at Lillegaard. And perhaps it's as well it was blown up. Since that happened, they will hardly connect us with the affair. Unless the guards should recognize you," he added anxiously.

Martin shook his head. "Ruggles dealt with the guards first. Sigurd's help came in afterward. Rug spoke some pretty emphatic English and is sure they will think it an English job. But what about Petra?" he asked. "Those officers quartered in our house—they had been in Halven, but they may have returned last night. And if they see her come home, out of the woods and through the garden, they may suspect something. She might be in a bad spot."

"Ole Haug took Petra with him," said Herr Roland reassuringly. "He had left his boat up the fjord a ways, and they planned to sail down the fjord to Valcos, fishing on the way."

Martin nodded, but the worried frown did not leave his face. "The work here is done for the time being," he said. "Petra and Mother may be in serious danger. I've got to get home and see how things are."

Herr Roland nodded. "If I were fifteen I am sure that is what I would do," he said. "But remember, Martin, use caution." He smiled and shook his head. "I keep saying that to you when I know it is almost asking the impossible. But this is dangerous and important business, and we don't know what lies ahead. Think before you act—that is as much as I can ask. Better be off without delay."

"Yes, sir," said Martin eagerly. "And I'll do my best to be cautious. I really will." They both laughed, for caution was not one of Martin's natural characteristics, but in these critical days he was trying hard to develop it.

Fru Roland herself packed a lunch for him, and he ate his sandwiches as he climbed the steep trail over the mountain. He was making his plans as he strode along. If only he could reach home before his sister did! Perhaps he might be able to, for he was taking the steep short cut, and she was going the long way around and would even stop to fish on the way home. She had been quick and clever enough to outwit the Nazis more than once, he reflected, and indeed— he smiled involuntarily as he thought of her—who would suspect her of plots and designs, a pretty little thing like Petra, looking much less than her fourteen years, with her big blue eyes and her soft curls tied up in a kerchief?

In the weeks that had passed since the Nazis came, both he and Petra had done plenty of things to aid the Norwegians—things that would have led to serious consequences if Captain Ebert had so much as suspected them. But nothing to compare in scope with last night's activities had been attempted before, and though Ruggles had done his best to make it look like an English job, Martin knew something of Nazi methods, and had no doubt that the matter would be thoroughly investigated. There was likely to be trouble ahead, and he hoped that he would at least get home in time to help his mother and sister, for he felt that all too likely help would be needed.

As he drew near home, he proceeded slowly and carefully, stopping to peer out from the shelter of the wood. The home garden lay quiet and peaceful in the morning sunshine, and he ventured toward it.

From the kitchen came cheerful sounds of activity, and good breakfast smells floated out of the open windows. So far, then, nothing serious had happened there. He had come in time. He went swiftly through the garden and put his finger on his lips as he entered the kitchen, for old Anna, their cook for as long as he could remember, started to cry out a welcome and almost dropped her pot of oatmeal.

"Petra home?" he asked, almost inaudibly.

Anna shook her head. "No, and so no fish for the officers' breakfast. I am sorry, for they are very cross," she whispered. "A good breakfast might put them in better humor."

"Where is Mother?" Martin continued in the same low tone.

"Upstairs. I heard her in her room a while ago."

Martin vanished silently up the back way, and Anna shook her head with a sigh as she remembered how he used to clatter up and down those stairs, especially if some of his favorite dishes were cooking. Now he hadn't so much as asked for a *baccle* or a piece of coffeecake.

His mother greeted him gladly. "O Martin! Thank God you are safe! But where is Petra?"

Martin told the story of their night's adventures in a few quick sentences. "Petra isn't home, then?" he asked anxiously. "I was hoping she would be here before me. Where are the officers?"

"In the study, talking. Messengers have come this morning with news which has upset them greatly. Now I know what it is—they have heard about Halven."

"Yes, and probably about the guns being taken from the caves where they had them hidden. I wish I could hear what they are saying," said Martin. Then he jumped up. "I know! That register in the ceiling that helps heat my room!"

"But your room is occupied by Otto. You can't possibly go and listen there," exclaimed his mother, her eyes big with anxiety. "No, Martin, you can't do that."

"But, Mother, I must. Otto's not there now, is he? You watch in the hall, and if you see or hear anything, just cough ever so little, and I'll manage to hide, in some way or other."

Without another word he stepped quickly across the hall to his own old room and lay flat on the floor with his ear to the register. The words came up to him indistinctly, and, though he knew German fairly well, it was difficult to follow the conversation as the messengers talked rapidly. He feared that his plan would not succeed after all. But then Captain Ebert began to speak, and not only did his deep voice carry better, but his German was much more like the book German Martin had learned at school.

"The Halven job—that's English, all right. The guards are sure of that, and it has all the earmarks. It is too clever for these dull Norwegians. But the guns taken from the caves—that's another matter. They love their guns, these Norwegians!"

"He's a fine one to say that," thought Martin wrathfully, and longed to shout his opinion right through the register. But Captain Ebert was speaking fast, and he had to concentrate to catch the words.

"We will have to find the ones responsible for that," he was saying harshly, "and deal with them accordingly!"

"Perhaps you remember, sir, the young girl who lives in this house has been absent much more than she should be," said Lieutenant von Berg. "She may know something about this."

"Ridiculous!" ejaculated the captain. "She only goes away to try to get something decent for us to eat—something for a change. A job like this would take real cleverness, and she almost borders on the stupid, poor child."

"I'm not sure she's as stupid as she acts," persisted Lieutenant von Berg. "Hans Torgerson, who has known them for years, looked quite surprised when I told him that."

"Well, you can see for yourself," said the captain sharply. "Her brother, now," he added, as a sudden thought struck him. "There's a different matter. He may well know something. We will get hold of him. He, I believe, could give us information. We'll try that. Otto!" he ordered. "Go to our hostess," and there was a sneer in his voice that made Martin clench his hands angrily. "Tell her to get word to her lout of a son to come home. We need him. At once! You need not quote my words exactly," he added.

Martin's face was white as he darted back across the hall, pushing his mother quickly into her room. "Mother," he explained swiftly, "they're sending Otto to ask for me. I'm going now, but tell them you'll try to see that I'm home sometime this afternoon."

As he had done often enough before, he stepped out of her window onto the sloping shed roof, and had barely gained the shelter of the big birch when he heard a sharp knock on his mother's door, Otto's gruff voice, and his mother's gentle: "Very well. Yes, I will try."

Then he swung himself down from the lowest limb and crept along as fast as he could in the shelter of the garden shrubs until he reached the woods above the house, for he had a plan, and he would have to work fast if he was to get everything ready and be back home before Captain Ebert grew too impatient. If only Sigurd were here to help him! Sig would know just what to do. His mind ran quickly over the boys left in and around Valcos. Eric Ostergaard, about his own age, was still here, as far as he knew, and Eric was brave and resourceful, he was sure of that, for they had often hunted and fished together and climbed the mountains. If he could just get hold of Eric!

More than once in these difficult days Martin had found their old birdcall signal of great use, and now, hidden in a small pine grove near Herr Dr. Ostergaard's, he gave the familiar whistle. At first no one seemed to notice, and his heart sank as two or three calls brought no response. Could it be that they had taken Eric to Halven, or had he managed, in spite of being only fifteen, to be put in one of the boats for England? How he could carry out his plan without Eric's help Martin couldn't see. Once again he pursed his lips for the call, and this time he almost shouted for joy, for here came Eric, walking carelessly as though going on some small errand. But Martin could see that his eyes were darting busily about. Eric too had learned to be cautious.

Once again Martin gave his call, and now Eric sauntered to the grove. Astonished though he was at Martin's presence there, he greeted him with enthusiasm and listened carefully as he talked. Then he grinned and nodded. "It's a wonderful plan—a little dangerous, though, I'd say. More than a little," he added soberly.

"I know that well enough. But what isn't these days?" demanded Martin. "Now, if you're with me on this, let's see if we can find Ole and Petra. I hope I haven't missed them."

The boys walked along, keeping carefully hidden among the rocks, and spent an anxious half hour looking vainly up the fjord for Ole's fishing boat. "We haven't the time to waste this way," fumed Martin. "You don't suppose they've been picked up, do you?"

"No, I don't think so. It's Ole's business to fish, you know, and that's what the Nazis want him to do. They need the fish. And Petra often goes with him," said Eric soothingly, for he was an even-tempered lad and well used to trying to ease things a bit for the more impulsive and high-spirited Martin. "Oh, here he comes, from down that way, and alone!" he said suddenly.

"Good! Good! That means he has got Petra safely home!" cried Martin, and added, with a grin, "in time so the officers had fish for breakfast, let us hope."

They were far enough up the shore by this time so that it was safe to call to Ole. At once the old

fisherman, who had learned to be surprised at nothing, put in to shore, picked the boys up, and listened
intently to Martin's plan, his face wrinkling in a wide
grin, his lips pursed in approval.

"We go straight there," he approved, nodding vigorously, "but first we stop at my house for two or three
guns. I had some old models the Nazis did not care to
take. They laughed when they saw them." Ole's face
grew suddenly grim. "But now we will have a use for
them, I see, and it may be our turn to laugh, though
not out loud."

It was late in the afternoon when Martin again
walked through his home garden. He would have been
there much earlier, but Ole had insisted that he stop
at his house for two or three hours' sleep. "You were
up all last night and a good share of the night before,"
he said. "And you have important business ahead. You
must be wide awake for that."

In vain Martin protested that he was too excited to
sleep, that Herr Roland had made him take some rest
the day before, and that he would sleep when it was all
over. Ole was firm.

"At least you try," he insisted. "I will wake you
in plenty of time." And indeed, hardly had Martin
stretched out when he was sound asleep. Now he was
glad of Ole's insistence, for his mind felt clear and
alert instead of weary and strained.

Petra, warned by Ole, was working in the garden,
and Martin managed to give her a few hasty directions before Otto, the orderly, came for him. "You
are to go at once to the study," he said gruffly. Once

before, Martin had slipped through Otto's fingers, but he was resolved that was not to happen again, and he marched the boy straight to the house.

"So! You are here!" Captain Ebert sat at Martin's father's desk and leaned back in the swivel chair.

It angered Martin to see this, but he was resolved to keep his wits about him, and he knew that in order to do that he had to keep a firm hold on his temper. So now he replied crisply, with a bow, "Yes, sir."

Captain Ebert turned to his desk, with his back to Martin. Then he swung around suddenly and barked out: "What do you know of those guns hidden in caves—stolen out of those caves by the Norwegians. You know about that, and you might as well tell all you know right now. It will be easier for all if you do."

Martin knit his brows and looked so bewildered that the captain hit the desk a hard blow with his fist. "Don't act as if you didn't know about it," he burst out angrily. "It's just the kind of thing a bunch of boys would think it was smart to do. But let me tell you, you may find the smart will be another kind. The best thing you can do now is to tell me all about it." He stopped for a moment. "Right now!" he shouted.

Martin stood silently looking down and seemed to be trying to decide what course to take.

"No use to be stubborn! We'll thresh this thing out, never fear!" There was a threat and a sneer in the captain's voice. He looked at Lieutenant von Berg, sitting beside the desk, and both of them laughed harshly.

"No fear of that!" echoed the lieutenant.

Petra, loitering near the study door, felt that this was her cue. She burst into the study, and without a glance at the officers darted to her brother's side. "O Martin!" she cried imploringly, "if you know anything about any cave where guns have been hidden, you'd better tell Captain Ebert. He'll find out anyway, and I can't bear—" Her voice broke, and Martin gave her hand a quick pat as he turned to the captain.

"Well, then, there is a cave," he began hesitantly, and Captain Ebert glanced triumphantly at the lieutenant. "Of course I can't say for sure whether it is the place, but it—well, it might be a likely one. Things have been hidden there in the past, I know."

"Can you take us to it?" asked the captain, satisfaction in his voice.

He had been prepared to deal severely with Martin, if need be, but this way was much better. Fru Engeland and Petra had managed to make him and his staff very comfortable, and he much preferred to keep on good terms with them, if possible.

Martin hesitated again, but Petra jogged his elbow and sent him a pleading glance.

"Yes, I think I can," he said slowly. "But it is not an easy climb," he warned them. "It is called Smugglers' Cave, and the name tells you it would be well hidden."

The captain looked somewhat uneasy, but he answered gruffly, "We are trained soldiers. We can certainly go anywhere a boy like you could go. Let us start at once. Come, Lieutenant! Come, Otto!"

Martin bowed and said, "I am ready, sir."

Never in all its centuries of use had Smugglers' Cave been reached by a more difficult route. Captain

Ebert was a trained soldier, no doubt of that, and so were the others, but they were not used to anything like Norwegian fjord shorelines, especially when their guide was a Norwegian lad who knew every crag and boulder along the way. It was not long before the captain was panting, his face red, his hands scratched and bruised.

"How far is this Smugglers' Cave?" he demanded, stopping to rest after a particularly difficult climb along the edge of a cliff.

"Oh, look out, sir!" cried Martin. "Hold on there!" The captain's red face grew quite white as he looked down from his precarious perch to the fjord waters far below.

"Oh, quite a way, sir. I told you it was not an easy climb," said Martin, managing to sound regretful, and glad that he was too far ahead for them to see the satisfaction he knew was in his eyes. "Here, I'll come back and give you a hand, sir."

The captain was silent, but he was breathing hard as Martin helped him over the worst bit. "At least I hope we find what we are looking for," he said, with a threat in his voice, when he was once again on safer footing.

"I hope so, sir," Martin replied respectfully, and started swiftly on again, longing to add that he was sure one member of the group, at least, would find exactly what he expected.

The party scrambled and climbed and slid in silence over the rocky ways, and at last Martin said: "We're almost there, sir. Do you think you can make it all right down that crag?"

He peered over the edge of the cliff, and glancing innocently back saw that the three Nazis were gazing down with alarm. "Do we go straight down that?" demanded the lieutenant.

"I'm afraid it's the only way to get there unless we want to go a very long way around," replied Martin. "I'll lead the way, if you wish."

"Well, go on!" ordered the captain harshly. "Don't stand around!"

Used as he was to the crags and cliffs and rocks, Martin went nimbly down, and the Nazis scrambled after him as well as they could. The captain's foot slipped on a rock, and he rolled down the last twenty feet. He picked himself up and stood, puffing and angry, at the foot of the crag. "Now show us that cave!" he exploded.

Silently Martin led the way, thankful that he and Eric and Ole had worked so hard and to such good purpose that morning, for now footsteps showed leading in and out of the sand at the edge of the cave, footsteps that led down the rocks to the fjord.

"This seems to be it!" he announced grimly.

"Yes, here we have it! Here are guns!" cried the lieutenant, flashing his torch into the cave's far corners, and Otto brought out to the light Ole's old guns that had been placed there that morning, when Ole and the two boys had tramped back and forth making the footprints.

Eagerly the captain seized them, and then threw them to the ground. "Old junk!" he cried angrily. "Old junk that even the Norwegians didn't care to take."

Ole's guns had served their purpose. The guns that the Nazis had scornfully rejected had done their work now for Norway.

"So then," said the captain slowly, thinking it out, "the Norwegians brought the guns here, all right, but they got them away. That was quick work for these dumb Norwegians. It only means we'll have to keep closer watch. We have been too lenient," he jerked out, looking angrily at Martin.

"They are quick enough to take advantage of that," said Lieutenant von Berg. "As you say, Captain, we will have to be far more stringent."

"Go and get us a boat, boy," barked the captain. "You know your way around here. Get us a boat. And quick!" A thought struck him and he looked at Martin in sudden suspicion, "Why didn't you bring us up by boat?"

But Martin was ready for that question. "There were none in the harbor, sir. And even if there had been, it takes an expert old sailor to come in the channel between those high rocks," he replied, glad that they had never seen him threading his way with his sailboat among the narrow, rocky islands along the Norwegian coast. "Even then there would have been the climb to the cave—almost sheer going," he added, looking at the cliff down which the captain had tumbled.

"All right, all right," said the captain impatiently. "But you'd better find a boat now, and a good sailor to sail it. And be quick about it!"

"Yes, sir," said Martin, thankful to get away, and eager to take the word to Ole.

They had expected that some such order would come, and Ole had promised to be somewhere in sight in his fishing boat. Martin hoped he would not be too far away. The captain's patience was very near the snapping point, he knew that. Thankfully he spied Ole some distance down the fjord, and Ole was watching for him.

"How did it work, boy?" demanded the old fisherman anxiously, as Martin stepped into the boat.

"It worked, Ole! They won't be looking for those guns anywhere else! They're convinced the guns were here all right, and have been spirited away. None of last night's workers will be in danger on account of those guns. Petra won't even be suspected. But they are mad as hornets that they didn't get here first, and we're going to have to be more careful than ever what we do from now on, and how we do it, Ole. They are going to tighten up and watch us like hawks, so it will be harder than ever to accomplish anything here. O Ole, I wish we could go to England! There's so much to do there, and I want to be at it."

"That will come," said Ole, and he stopped rowing for just a moment to put his hand on Martin's shoulder. "But, boy, you've done a man's work, and better, in the last two days, and there is more ahead for you to do." He hesitated, and then spoke with a slow emphasis that steadied the boy's impatient spirit. "Big work, Martin. I doubt if we can get many more boats off from this neighborhood. Yet many young men want to get off to England for training. Word has already got around secretly that we can help. We must find ways." His tone changed as he said cheerfully, "This afternoon's adventure and its success should put heart in all of us."

"Yes, I liked that—leading the captain around the hard way," agreed Martin, and in spite of himself a grin broke out. "I guess you're right, Ole. My job is here for right now."

"Good boy!" approved Ole. "You wait! We'll get you off to England yet. But now here we go to get the captain and take him a safe, comfortable trip home. And remember," his faded blue eyes twinkled, and the smile wrinkles around them were deep as he looked at Martin, "no rocking the boat!"

XV

Martin Turns Messenger

T HE LITTLE COMPANY in Ole's sailboat made a quiet trip down the fjord. Captain Ebert was stiff and sore from his unaccustomed climb, and worse still he had the uncomfortable feeling that perhaps he had been outwitted by these courteous and apparently co-operative Engelands. He had had the feeling once or twice before, and he more than half suspected that it was fully shared by Lieutenant von Berg. Yet there was nothing he could put his finger on.

Martin and Ole were absorbed in their sailing, for a wind had come up and the sky looked stormy. Ole shouted his directions in Norwegian, which Captain Ebert did not understand, and which he therefore suspected.

Once Martin broke into an irresistible laugh and Captain Ebert said sharply: "This is no time for jokes. That sky looks stormy, and I've heard these fjords are treacherous."

"That's true indeed, sir," replied Martin, sobering instantly.

For one delectable moment he toyed with the idea of upsetting the boat and landing the whole company in the water. But he remembered regretfully Ole's laughing instructions not to rock the boat, and he realized that, in spite of his apparent co-operation, he had done quite enough today to harass the captain. They made a safe and speedy passage, for the wind was in their favor, and soon the little craft docked at the home pier.

Martin could not help laughing, in spite of the seriousness of the situation, as he regaled his mother and sister with the story of the afternoon's experiences.

"You should have seen Captain Ebert puffing and panting," he chuckled, "and even Lieutenant von Berg was pretty red in the face. Of course I took them over Gunnar's Peak, and that isn't a very good road, though it's shorter, which I would have explained if he had asked me."

"Martin," said Petra a little anxiously, "you don't think the captain suspects you of leading him a merry chase—"

"And certainly you don't think he has any idea of what you did last night and this morning," whispered his mother. "O son, I'm going to breathe far more easily when you're back at Lillegaard."

"Yes, and I've got to get there in a hurry. We have a lot to do there, and fast. If they inquire for me, just say that this is the time we usually go on our hike, and we never plan the destination. But, O ladies!" he burst out again, smiling broadly and eager to bring back a smile to his mother's anxious face, "never did I wish so for my camera as when those fellows were clambering over Gunnar's Peak. That would have been one for the Camera Club at Lillegaard to laugh over. They went like this!" Martin, using the bed for a mountain, began clumsily to illustrate; and in spite of themselves they laughed so that Petra had to clamp both fists against her mouth to stifle the sound.

But the laugh was cut short by a sharp knock, and Petra, answering it, found Otto standing there. He clicked his heels together and delivered his message: "Your brother. Captain Ebert wants him in the study at once. Come with me."

The laughter in their eyes changed to a look of sick fear, and Petra swallowed hard before she could reply, "Very well."

Martin gave his mother a glance which he intended to be encouraging, and he knew she was trying to send the same kind of look back at him. But all of them felt this summons could mean only one thing. The captain had concluded that Martin knew of the events of the night before, and he intended to get the information out of him. And all of them knew that the Nazis had their own methods of doing this, and were not delicate about using them.

Petra made an attempt to go with him, but this time Otto blocked her so decidedly that she could not pretend to misunderstand. "Not you. Your brother," he said very clearly.

As Martin marched down the stairs, with Otto following, he tried to collect his thoughts, tried to formulate some plausible answers to questions about last night's activities. His mouth was dry, and he clenched his hands hard. He was determined that he would not break down before these Nazis.

Captain Ebert was, as usual, sitting in Martin's father's big swivel chair at the desk with Lieutenant von Berg close by. For some reason, Martin felt more afraid of the lieutenant than he did of the captain. Now the captain swung around and sat for a moment saying nothing, only looking the boy over from head to foot. Martin managed to stand the examination with dignity, his head high, his eyes straight ahead.

At last the captain said slowly, "Martin Engeland, we have something you must do for us."

The tone was not unfriendly, but that put Martin even more closely on his guard. The captain went on: "At first we did not know how to make you out. Your mother and sister had been kind and courteous. But you—we did not know where you stood, and the lieutenant here and I myself were somewhat suspicious of you. We watched you rather carefully. But your willing co-operation this afternoon proved that you wish to be helpful. We see now that you understand what we wish all your countrymen understood, that we Germans don't want trouble with you Norwegians. All we are doing is for your own good."

It was one of the hardest things Martin had ever done not to make a scornful reply to this speech. But he set his teeth together hard and stood there, outwardly respectful, inwardly seething. What could the captain be leading up to? Surely he didn't think Martin was in sympathy with the Nazis. But apparently he did, for he went on smoothly, the tips of his fingers pressed together as he rocked back and forth comfortably in Captain Engeland's chair.

"We have an important message to be taken to Halven. You must deliver it there to someone I am sure you know, a fine Norwegian boy named Hans Torgerson, who has been most co-operative." He watched Martin closely as he spoke. "What do you say?"

Martin's mind was racing, and he had come to a swift conclusion. Certainly he would do this. It would give him the very opportunity he wanted to talk to Hans again. And perhaps he could even make this fit in with his plans. He realized clearly that it would go hard with him if he pretended to side with them and later they discovered their mistake. It was the very thing of which he had warned Hans.

"Certainly I will take your message for you," he replied, with a bow. "And may I ask then that I be allowed to go on and finish out the school year? It is our custom to have a special hike, and there are various other activities."

The captain thought for a moment. "I see no objection to that," he said "I well remember what those schoolboy hikes meant to me."

Martin, recalling the afternoon's activities, wondered a little about those schoolboy hikes of the captain's.

"When you have delivered the message, telephone that it was safely received. I don't wish to telephone the message, for reasons you can easily understand, but you may phone here and say simply, "Safe journey.""

You can give that message to your sister, and if anyone is listening in, no one will suspect that you have done anything unusual. They will think you are phoning of your own safety. She will give the message to me. Give her that direction."

"Yes, sir," said Martin, and waited while the captain wrote his message and sealed it. Then he took it and marched back upstairs, feeling as though he were dreaming.

"You are sure that is safe? You think he is a good messenger?" he heard the lieutenant say in a low voice.

"Absolutely," returned the captain, and the fact that he left the study door half open indicated that he meant what he said. "These Engelands are somewhat puzzling, I know that, yet they are useful in many ways. In time we might even get the co-operation of the father, and that would be a good thing indeed, well-liked and influential as he is. And Martin is much brighter than his mother and sister. A bright, willing Norwegian boy can be very helpful."

"I realize that," murmured the lieutenant. "Shut that door, Otto." But before it was shut Martin heard him say, "I wonder if he's just a little too bright and willing."

"Do you suspect everyone, Lieutenant?" demanded the captain impatiently. "Give some folks credit for a little sense. These Norwegians aren't all fools."

Fru Engeland and Petra listened in wonder to his story, and when he had finished his sister burst out: "Oh, I don't like this, Martin! I don't like it at all. The whole thing looks like a trap to me." Her eyes were anxious as she looked at her brother. "Do you have to do it, Martin? Haven't you done enough?"

"It's never enough till the whole job is done," he shot back. "You know that, Petra, just as well as I do." But he patted her shoulder gently and added: "You've proved it, and you've certainly run into plenty of danger. You wouldn't want me to hold back now, would you, at this critical time?"

"No, of course not," answered Petra, but her voice trembled a little. "It's the captain acting so cordial that has me worried. He's been so—well, so sharp with you. And now acting so friendly, sending you to Hans Torgerson—it doesn't look good to me. I'm going to be on the watch, Martin, and don't be surprised if I suddenly turn up in Lillegaard."

"I wouldn't be much surprised at anything you did, sister. I'm about through being surprised at you," returned Martin, and they both smiled. "But be a little careful, won't you, Petra?" he urged. "I'm glad to have you on the watch, but don't be in too much of a hurry to come to Lillegaard. That might be a very dangerous trip for you now. But it's a trip I'd better be getting started on right away," he added in a lighter tone. "Don't you agree, Mother?"

Fru Engeland waited a moment before she spoke, and both of them knew well that she was trying not to show too much anxiety. She gave a deep-drawn sigh, and in spite of her effort her voice was not quite steady as she said: "We're walking on thin ice, Martin. Pray God it holds."

"If we're careful it will hold, Mother," said Martin, squeezing her hand hard. "At least while we need it. Now I'm off."

"And if there are any new developments here, I'll get word to you somehow," said Petra firmly.

"I know I can depend on that, all right," replied her brother. "Good-by now."

As he climbed over the mountain, Martin could hardly keep his hands off the sealed packet he was carrying. Perhaps Hans would know some way of opening it.

But Hans, surprised as he was to find Martin acting as messenger, took the envelope in silence. "It goes to Julius Staeck," he said, after a moment's examination of it. "I've had these for him before—he has a code name. He works with the lame man, and Kurt, of course, and he handles hardware and messages and such for the head of the plant. He's a sort of go-between, general utility man. I'll find out what's in it, if I can. Now, how did you get into this business? I don't like that, Martin. Too dangerous."

"I know that," answered Martin. "I don't like it myself." In a few words he explained the situation. Then he added impulsively: "Hans, if you see trouble ahead for yourself, or for any of us, get to Lillegaard. I'm going to tell Herr Roland what you are doing. Someone besides me should know. The time has come for that."

Hans thought hard and then nodded slowly. "You may be right," he agreed. "It would be a relief to me, I needn't tell you. It looks to me as if there's trouble ahead, and not far off. It might be necessary then for

Herr Roland to know he could trust me. But I'll stick it here as long as I can."

"It's a bad spot," said Martin, with a steady look of appreciation, "but you're doing a real job here, one of the hardest."

"Thanks," said Hans in a low tone. "It's a help, Martin, that you know what I'm doing. Go, now, do your phoning and be on your way. They may be watching us even now." He hesitated and added, very low: "Martin, listen! Look out for the lame man. He's back here. And tell Herr Roland the same. I saw him prowling around the ruins of the school. And Kurt was with him."

"You look out for him too," said Martin, and was off.

In the little study at Lillegaard, Herr Roland greeted him with a hearty handshake and a relieved: "Martin! I'm glad you're here. We didn't know if you'd make it back."

"Oh, yes, sir! We've got to get to work on that secret passage, you know." Quickly Martin told the story of the day's adventures, winding up with Hans's warning.

"The lame man!" echoed Herr Roland. "I thought he had moved on elsewhere in the plane he took. Prowling around the ruins of the school! Well, he wouldn't find much, but still I don't like that, Martin. It shows he is suspicious of us."

Martin looked grave. "I'm afraid Hans is in danger, too. And this errand they sent me on may even be a trap." He shook himself and jumped up, anxious to be at work. "This is usually the time we take our hike. Why don't we older boys get right to work, instead, on that secret passage?"

"Tonight?" asked Herr Roland, smiling a little. "When do you intend to sleep, boy?"

"I slept this afternoon," returned Martin, "but I suppose we can't do much until the younger boys have been sent home. We don't want many people around when we begin that work. It may prove to be very important."

"I've dispatched most of the younger pupils and some of the older ones to their homes today," said the professor. "Families heard of the blowing up of Halven School, and anyone who could get here did, of course. I am glad to have that over. For one thing I'm glad to have the younger pupils in their homes. And the fewer people around here now the better, Martin, for Lillegaard is becoming an important center. The point is, we don't want people to know how important it is."

Martin nodded. "Who's left?" he asked.

"Gunnuf Olson, Johann Berg—"

Suddenly Martin jerked his head up, his face alert. "What was that?" he whispered.

Across the porch came a halting step, and both of them turned white as they listened.

"The lame man!" breathed Martin, for once unable to force himself into action. Both of them sat rigid, shoulders hunched forward.

Then Herr Roland rose, stood for a moment very still and straight, and walked to the door. As he threw it wide, someone fairly fell into the room, someone greeted by Martin and the professor with muffled cries of surprise, of alarm, of concern. For it was not the lame man who entered in this strange way, but one of the young masters who had left in the boats for England.

"Peter! Peter Nybroten!" they exclaimed, and bent to his aid. "We thought you were in England. How did you get here?"

"Our boat was shot at and sunk before we had gone far," Peter mumbled. "I was wounded, but I swam and swam and swam—" his words trailed off. "I managed to get to shore. Hope some of the others did. Got here—" his voice faded out again.

"Martin, quick! Call Fru Roland. She is a good nurse. He needs food and care. And we will get him into the cellar. They may be following him."

Quickly but carefully Peter Nybroten was moved to a dry, warm cot underground. Fru Roland, shaking her head and folding her lips very tight, as she did when she was angry, dressed his wounds and brought him hot broth. "This first, more later. How long since you have eaten?"

"Three days," he admitted, and managed, in spite of his weakness, to smile at her. "Oh, I hope the other fellows were as lucky as I."

"We must find a better way than the open boats," burst out Martin. "We must find a better way to get you fellows out of the country—one that is safer. We must find places to hide and care for the ones who have to come back, if we can—places where the ones ready to go can wait their chance. Even here it isn't safe for Peter. If they searched Lillegaard they would find him."

"We'll get him to the cave where the guns are as soon as we can. He'll be safe there. But we can't take him outdoors, you know," said Herr Roland, troubled and anxious, "and the other way isn't cleared yet."

"No!" Weak as he was, Peter sat straight up. Then he dropped back. "They may be following me," he panted. "I've put you all in danger. Oh, I should not have come! But I didn't know where else to go. What's that?" he whispered in sudden alarm.

For a second time that night, halting steps scraped across the porch and stopped at the door. There were other steps too, firm and heavy.

Fru Roland's head jerked up angrily at the pounding on the door. "Someone should teach them manners!" she exclaimed. "I will fix them."

"Open! Open here! Open, or we batter in the door!" came the loud threat.

Martin glanced swiftly from Herr Roland to Peter. The young master's eyes were wide with fear, but he was struggling to get off his cot, "I can't put you in danger," he said, and now his voice was firm. "I will give myself up. I will say that I forced my way in here—that I fooled you—"

"Nonsense! You'll do nothing of the kind," said Fru Roland coolly. "I'll go up and deal with them. I'll give you as much time as I can." And she ran briskly up the stairs, her gray curls bobbing.

"I'm afraid I must go too," said the professor. "Maybe I can satisfy them in some way—keep them from coming down. But what about you boys?"

"We'll manage," said Martin swiftly. "It may be you can keep them away from here, for a while, at least. Listen to them! They mean business."

"I'll have to hurry," said Herr Roland, for sounds of a loud conversation were heard through the thick flooring, and a harsh voice shouted: "You'll harbor no fugitives here! You'll hide no dangerous equipment! We demand to search the house from garret to cellar!"

 XVI

The Cave at Lillegaard

MARTIN, LEFT ALONE in the cellar with Peter, looked wildly around. Surely there must be some small hiding place. There were piled-up boxes, true enough, and several doors led to storage closets, but it was of no use to think of trying to hide anyone there. Those would be the very places the Nazis would look first.

He glanced despairingly at Peter, and then sprang toward him, for Peter was struggling to get off his couch, and his face was grim and resolute. "Herr Roland whispered as he passed me—third door in that wall—big stone—press twice," he panted.

Martin sped to investigate. The door opened easily enough, but it offered nothing more than the other closets. Big stone—why the whole place was lined with big stones! One after another he pressed the biggest ones, and at last one yielded a little under his hands. His heart was pounding, and he heard Peter's dragging feet close behind him. Again he gave a firm double pressure, and the stone moved.

"Peter, it's the way to the secret passage all right," whispered Martin, and soon he had the opening big enough so that he could help Peter through. "Now I must take care of that cot, fast, and get out of sight myself. If I don't make it, Peter, you must manage to push that stone shut. They mustn't find out about the secret passage."

He flew back to the main cellar, stood the cot upright against the walls as if it belonged there, and made a rough bundle of the bedding.

The Rolands had delayed the Nazis to good purpose, so much was clear, but now the heavy steps were coming this way, and Martin had just time to dart into the closet, close the door, wriggle through the opening with the bedding, and push the stone back into place. He sank down in the passage feeling almost as weak as Peter, as through the thick wall came muffled sounds of searching.

He and Peter could hear voices, the Nazis' guttural speech, their tones angry and chagrined, Herr Roland's suave answering tones. But then came a voice, higher pitched and more easily understood.

Fru Roland was saying, in German: "You have found something, no? Ah, you are disappointed. Let me at least give you some coffee for your trouble."

Martin chuckled softly, and Peter whispered, "She's a great one!" Both of them knew well Fru Roland's brisk common sense and love of fun.

"She's like a mischievous little boy right now, but she'll do her job just the same," murmured Martin. "She is going to have a fine time pulling the wool over their eyes. They won't search Lillegaard again for a long time. I only wish we could have those cookies she's going to feed them."

But Peter didn't answer. Now that the danger was temporarily over, both for himself and for his friends, and he no longer had to brace himself to an effort, he slumped down, thoroughly exhausted.

"Peter, don't faint!" implored Martin, far more panicky at this possibility than he had been at the coming of the Nazis. "I'm spreading a bed for you right here, and then I'm going to investigate this passage. I won't be gone long."

Peter stretched out thankfully and Martin set off. It was slow going, for he had neither flashlight nor candle, and there was thick darkness in the passage, but he was extremely anxious to find out how far he could go before the way was blocked. If they were to use the great cave for hiding fugitives, as well as for storing guns, the way to it must be cleared, and without delay.

The passage was very old and very narrow. His hands, touching each side, told him that it had been hewn from solid rock. "The Norwegians have been in trouble before," he thought to himself. "It must have been serious trouble that made them hew out such a place as this. But we've always come through before, and we will this time."

At last, however, he came to a place where the stone had crumbled and fallen and blocked the way, and he turned back, eager to tell Herr Roland what he had found. There would not be so much work here as he had feared, and a good thing too. For now he knew that there was other work of importance which must be done without delay—a new way must be found to get men and boys out of the country—Peter must get out as soon as he was well enough; Hans might have to leave at any moment. He himself, he felt sure, was far from safe. And what of his mother and Petra?

A faint light was shining down the passage as he neared the opening. Herr Roland was there, and together they soon had Peter comfortably ensconced on the cot.

"How did you get rid of them so soon?" asked Martin.

"It was that wife of mine," chuckled the old professor. "I wish you could have heard her. So sympathetic as she was with the Nazis! *Ja, Ja!*" He clucked his tongue and shook his head in such a comical imitation of his clever little wife that both boys laughed. "So much good advice she gave them of places to look where they will find nothing. She talked so fast and laughed so hard that they were thoroughly bewildered. I am sure they thought her more than a little crazy. They ate very fast, and left as soon as they could. I think they will not return right away. They didn't seem to like Lillegaard very well. And yet how helpful the little Fru Roland was—she was running in front of them all the time, eager to show everything, not getting in their way more than a dozen times, especially of the lame man and that old Julius Staeck!"

"She's a wonder!" said Martin, laughing heartily as he pictured the whole affair.

"Yes, she is," agreed a merry voice, and Fru Roland herself came down the stairs with a tray in her hands. "If I can give food to the Nazis, I am not going to neglect my brave Norwegians," she said, and in the flickering candlelight, the four sat in the old cellar talking and planning as they ate their midnight feast.

"A route over the border to Sweden—that's what you have in mind." All of them had been thinking this, but it was Fru Roland who spoke the words aloud. "This would be a safe starting place now, I think, for a while at least."

They were all agreed that the first job was to open the secret passage into the cave. That would provide safe hiding for those who needed it, in a place where it would be possible to live not too uncomfortably for a few days until the next hiding place could be reached.

"From here to Sturm Cave, perhaps. Not even Kurt knows that one, and we boys know a trail very little-used, very difficult, but a good Norwegian could make it," said Martin. "Gunnuf and Johann and I could act as guides, any of us, and some of the other boys as well. But I don't quite see the next step."

"My uncle has a farm near the Swedish border," offered Peter eagerly. "He would help us, I am sure, if we could find a good way. But how would we get there?"

"Those are the things we have to figure out," said Herr Roland, "and I think we can do it."

"And while we're doing that," said Martin, "we'll be working on that passage."

Through the next days the boys worked, clearing away piles of sand and crumbled stone. At last, late one evening, they found themselves at the entrance of the big cave where the guns were stored.

They had expected to find Peter there, for he had been shifted to that safe hiding place some nights before. But they had expected to find him alone, and as they opened the low door and entered the cave, Martin gave an exclamation of surprise, for the Rolands were there too, and seated in the midst of the group, and talking fast and very earnestly, was his sister Petra.

She sprang up and flew to Martin, and in spite of his dirty and disheveled condition, she threw her arms around him and clung close to him for a moment.

He could feel that she was trembling, and he knew she was struggling to keep from bursting into tears. "Why, Petra—" he began, surprised by this unusual conduct on the part of his self-reliant little sister.

But she interrupted him in great agitation: "O Martin! I was right about it! You are in great danger! Oh, how glad I was to find you were safe underground! You must stay here. They can't lay hands on you here! Shut that door, won't you?"

"They'd never find this little door way at the end of the corridor," said Gunnuf reassuringly. "We had a hard enough time to find it ourselves." But he shut it promptly, for Petra was a great favorite and all of them longed to help her now.

"Why, Petra!" Martin said again, but his tone was very gentle. "After all the things you've done—all the dangers you've been through—you're not going to pieces now!"

"But it wasn't you who was in danger before—" burst out Petra, her voice half breaking on a sob.

It was Fru Roland who broke in, in her brisk way: "Of course she isn't going to pieces! A girl like Petra? What do you take her for?"

"I take her for a brave Norwegian girl," said Herr Roland quietly. "That's what she has more than once proved herself to be, and she'll do it again. Her job is cut out for her."

Petra looked gratefully from one of the Rolands to the other, gave an angry dash at her eyes with her handkerchief, cleared her throat, swallowed hard, and said firmly: "You can just count on that. We'll get Martin out of this."

"But what is it?" asked Martin, thoroughly bewildered. "I thought I left on good terms with the captain."

"Well, I didn't think so. I suspected that Lieutenant von Berg," said his sister, with an indignant jerky nod. "We might have managed the captain. Do you know what was in that message you took to Hans? It was the order that brought the men here to search Lillegaard."

"Peter had managed to throw them off his trail, weak as he was," said Herr Roland proudly. "They probably would have come here sooner or later, for they suspected us of harboring runaway Norwegians and about everything else, but it was that message that brought them here so soon. The lame man and perhaps Kurt had sent word to Captain Ebert—"

"They'd been prowling among the ruins of the school," Fru Roland explained scornfully, "and they'd found some of the photographic equipment used by the Camera Club. They thought we'd been taking pictures of their precious plant, and perhaps other things of theirs. It gives us an idea," she added cheerfully, "we might just do that. Well, that was why they hunted around the cellar so hard and opened all the closets. Thought we were setting up another darkroom, and they'd find some incriminating evidence. As if we were that stupid!"

"They knew some of the men had got to shore, too, and undoubtedly they thought we might be entertaining them here," said Herr Roland. "You heard what they said about 'fugitives.'"

"They expected to make a haul of some kind, all right," said Peter.

"Hans found out about this and got word to me by Ole Haug, who has made it his business to be over in Halven whenever he could," explained Petra. "The lame man said to Hans: 'You're much smarter than that Engeland boy. You're smart enough to work with us for the good of your country. He had his chance, but we know well enough that he's up to no good. We're just giving him enough rope to hang himself, and he'll do it fast enough—hang himself and some others too, we're sure of that. Maybe we'll find him doing something that will force us to pick him up at Lillegaard. It would be comical if he were picked up by a message he himself brought.'"

Martin's face was white and grim, but his arm tightened reassuringly around his sister for a moment before he turned to Herr Roland and said, in a strained voice: "Well, it seems I am no further use here. Rather a detriment, for they suspect me and may trace others by me. I must have bungled somewhere."

"Martin! You haven't bungled!" cried his sister. "Perhaps you have a bigger job than ever ahead of you. Perhaps you will be the first one to leave by the new route you are planning."

A look of eagerness chased away the chagrined expression on Martin's face. "That's right!" he cried. "I wish Peter could go too. There should be two of us. Oh, if only we could start soon!"

Herr Roland put his hand on the boy's shoulder. "So far you have done well, Martin. You have kept your promise to be cautious, and I know it has not been easy. Now you must be patient too. First of all, we must make better plans and preparations. That may take a little time. By then there may be others to go."

"And in the meantime, Martin, you stay right here with Peter," ordered Fru Roland briskly. "And, Petra, can you get back over the mountain tonight so as to be home when the officers awake in the morning?"

"Oh, no," burst out Martin, "she can't do that."

"Of course I can," said Petra, with a half-scornful chuckle. "Martin, don't worry. That's just nothing after some of the things I've had to do. I intended that all along. I wouldn't dare stay away. We're under too much suspicion."

"But how will I get word to you?" demanded Martin. "O Petra, I wish we had that sending station you've been wishing for."

"From Lillegaard to Valcos? That wouldn't be a very secret station for long, I'm afraid," said Herr Roland, smiling a little.

"No, I see that now," said Petra. "I've wished for a radio sending station, but I can see it wouldn't be practical at all—not now, at least. But Ole Haug did have a practical idea," she went on eagerly. "You know those pigeons he took such care of? Two of them are homing pigeons. He was saving them for a great emergency, and he thinks this is it. They are upstairs in a basket. We must see you, Martin, if we can, before you go." She had to stop to steady her voice. "There may be important messages for you to take. If there is any other desperate need, send a message."

Martin nodded, for when he thought of how long it might be before they would see each other again, and how much might happen in the meantime, his throat felt tense and full of an ache that kept him from speaking.

"Now I'm going," said Petra, keeping her head down as she gave him a quick hug, for there were tears in her eyes and she didn't want her brother to see them.

"I'm going with you," said Gunnuf, and the other boys looked as if they wished they had said it first.

But Petra shook her head. "No, thank you. One alone is not so easily seen, and I get around these mountains as quiet as a weasel now. And if you weren't seen going, you might be seen returning. Right now we have to keep Lillegaard looking as innocent as a baby. Big doings here, you know." But she threw a smile at all of them over her shoulder as she went out with Fru Roland.

Martin, lying wide awake that night on his cot in the great cave, stared into the darkness and tried to plan an escape route. From here to Sturm Cave. So much was fairly simple. There was a brook there. One could hide for some days if necessary. He knew where the Nybroten farm lay—well over toward the Swedish border. It was in a thickly-wooded country, partly surrounded by forests. That would be a help, a great help. But two mountain ridges blocked the way, and a long stretch of valley land beside a river. They were used to mountains. They could negotiate those, but the valley road was the part of the route that was making the deep, anxious line between Martin's eyes. One plan after another came to his mind. The Holms' upper farm, where Sigurd's father and uncle were at work, lay near that road. They would soon be haying, if indeed they were not already doing so. Perhaps they could smuggle some travelers out in a load of hay—the first ones, at least. It was only a chance. They might be challenged, of course. Martin realized that his method had been tried before, sometimes successfully, sometimes unsuccessfully. He remembered hearing that searching bayonets had been thrust deep into loads of hay. There was the river too. Perhaps a boat with a small secret compartment could take one or two at a time. No doubt, among them, they could manage to find ways to cross that valley. They must find ways. There was no "perhaps" about it.

He was anxious too about Petra. That climb over the mountain at night—they shouldn't have let her go. Even if it was risky for her to stay, everything was risky these days. He wished that she were safe here. She was such a fine one too, to help to plan.

Petra, for her part, was longing for Martin's companionship as she climbed the steep trail alone. Even though it was not very dark, mountain noises were terrifying at night. And that lame man, Hartsell, seemed to be everywhere. He it was who was going around the mountains, to the saeters, finding out where the flocks and herds were, already commandeering some, getting ready to confiscate others. And Kurt was helping—helping to harm and to take food from the Norwegians, after all they had done for him. She was planning now, as fiercely as Martin, but her plans were ways to rid Norway of Kurt and the lame man. Perhaps Sig and Ruggles could seize them and take them in a plane to England. Perhaps Ole could help to smuggle them out in a boat. If only they could be got out of the country, Martin would have a far better chance to make a safe getaway.

When she was almost home, she stopped, as she always did now, to look down from the shelter of the wood before she ventured out. Home had always been such a refuge, but now it had become more of a menace. Father could not return there now, and neither could Martin. As she stood there a moment, her mother came stealing out of the back door into the garden, looking anxiously toward the wood. Something in her attitude told Petra plainly that this was not the first time that early morning that she had stolen out to look.

Without another moment's delay Petra dashed out of the wood and started running down the path. But she stopped short as her mother, with a quick, decided gesture, motioned her back toward the wood. The girl turned swiftly and darted back into its shelter, wondering what this could possibly mean. Mother would surely be here in a moment with the explanation. She turned expectantly, sure that she would see her mother walking swiftly up the hill. But her heart seemed to come right up into her throat, for there was no one on the hill, no one in the home garden. Fru Engeland had disappeared.

It seemed a long moment that Petra stood there, waiting and watching. Then at last her mother reappeared with a large bundle. She began toiling up the hill, not walking with her usual brisk step, but slowly, as if she were carrying a heavy burden. Petra longed to run and help her, but that quick, commanding gesture kept her where she was.

Now she had reached the wood, and Petra hurried down the path to meet her. "Mother, what is it?" she asked anxiously.

"Petra," gasped Fru Engeland, "Captain Ebert suspects us—has found out something. We are all in danger—you and I and Martin. We must get away, all of us, if it's not too late."

XVII

Fugitives on the Mountain

"WHAT HAPPENED, MOTHER? Where are we going? Have you any plan?" Petra asked, as the two of them hurried along the woodland path. She had taken part of her mother's bundle, and with the load divided they made good time, for Fru Engeland was plainly determined to get far away from Valcos with all possible speed.

"They were doing so much talking in the study, Petra. Talking and laughing. Then the lame man came, and Kurt. I knew it was important. I listened at the register in Martin's room. The lame man talked a great deal. He said they must get hold of Martin. He had been seen in too many suspicious places. They have been watching him. The lame man had seen him at the saeter—suspected him of working with Sigurd and Ruggles."

"Why did they let him go free then?" asked Petra. "They had him right there."

"They intended to let him get himself in deeper—do more things—try to find out some of the others working with him. Then they would hold him, and

223

through him would work on your father to give up what he is doing. I find Father is doing extremely important work, Petra. They are anxious to bring pressure on him. That is why we must get away. They would hold us as hostages."

"They don't suspect me of doing anything at all?" Petra demanded.

"You have them puzzled. The lame man and the lieutenant are a little suspicious of you, but Kurt and the captain laughed at them. They really like you, Petra. The captain chuckled and sounded almost friendly when he spoke of you. That is one of the things that has helped most."

"But where are we going? Do we dare to go to Lillegaard? I hate to do that. They may be following us even now. We mustn't bring suspicion there. It's such an important place now."

"No, we can't go there. Maybe we will just have to hide in a cave. That's why the bundle is so heavy. I brought food in case we have to hide several days. I brought extra clothing under my skirts too, besides this bundle of coats. That is why I am so awkward in my walking. We had to be ready. But where we are going I don't know."

A summer rain had begun to fall, and that made the going more difficult. Petra could see that her mother's face was white and very weary. She longed to get her to a place of safety.

"Mother, we could go to the Holm saeter. They have a sort of secret closet where they store bedding and things in the winter. You get to it through a trap door. It's not large, but we could hide there for a little while, if necessary."

"I wouldn't want to bring them trouble—" began Fru Engeland, but Petra broke in.

"Mother, they're Norwegians too. They'd want to help all they could. But I sort of doubt if they are being watched. The Nazis wouldn't think even we would be stupid enough to go back there after all that has happened."

Fru Engeland raised her hand warningly, and lifted her head, listening intently. "We're being followed," she whispered, almost inaudibly. Her eyes were full of terror, and Petra's heart beat so hard she could scarcely breathe. Their thoughts flew to Father, and what it would mean for him if they were taken as hostages. They looked wildly around for some kind of hiding place.

At the other side of the trail, clinging precariously to the edge of the precipice, was a thick clump of bushes, and they crept swiftly over and concealed themselves there. "Hold tight," whispered Petra, and her mother nodded, for both of them knew that this was a dangerous hiding place. If they lost their hold, or a bit of the cliff gave way, they would plunge over the precipice, and the rain made their hold the more slippery.

They could hear steps coming up the trail toward them, uneven steps, but swift, and heavier steps behind them. Petra's mouth was dry. It was the lame man and Kurt again. They must have been watching even more closely than she had feared.

"They wouldn't come up here again," Kurt was saying. "They wouldn't take a chance like that."

"I'm not so sure," rasped the lame man. "They don't know which way to turn. There aren't many ways to get out of this Valcos, and they seem to realize how serious it would be if they were taken. They know their friends up here would do anything to help them—fools that they are. It will be their turn next, when I tell my tale where it will do the most good." He paused, almost beside their clump of bushes, and looked searchingly around. "Are you keeping a close watch as you go? They're smart, you know, smart enough to outwit the captain, and that makes him furious!" Hartsell laughed unpleasantly. "They may be hiding right around here some place. I don't care to spend this whole day trudging around these mountains in the rain."

In the very riskiness of the fugitives' position lay their safety, for nobody would have suspected that they would dare take refuge in that clump of bushes on the very edge of the cliff. But not until the lame man and Kurt were out of sight and even out of hearing, did Petra and her mother edge their way back to the comparative safety of the trail.

"Oh!" said Petra, with a long-drawn sigh of relief. "I held my breath most of that time, Mother."

"And now we must find a safer place to hide," said Fru Engeland, "for they may be back this way. A dry place if we can, Petra."

"There's a cave not much farther on up the mountain, some way off this trail. I don't think even Kurt knows it. Inga and I found it last year. We used to go there for shelter when a sudden rain would come up while we were tending the cattle."

"Let's go there, just as fast as we can," exclaimed her mother.

Down in the cave at Lillegaard, Martin paced restlessly back and forth. For the first time, he felt absolutely trapped. Things had been dangerous enough before, but he could always see at least a little way ahead. Now he could not see one step. If only they had had a few days to prepare that new route of escape! Through the night he had thought and planned, and at last he had thought he saw a possible way. But how could they make necessary arrangements? Herr Roland, under heavy suspicion, could not make them now, nor could any of the Halven boys. Peter, of course, was far from ready to give any assistance. For a short time the night before, the two had talked and tried to plan, but in the very midst of it Peter had fallen asleep from utter exhaustion.

There were Ole's homing pigeons, of course, but he felt those must be saved for an extreme emergency. He knew well enough that when that message was sent, Petra and his mother were only too likely to take action that would lead them straight into danger. His great fear now, indeed, was that they were already un-der suspicion, since he was. That was the chief cause of his restless anxiety. Here he was, worried and mis-erable, but safe; and there was no telling what danger they were in right at this moment. He felt he just had to get out of here and do something.

"Here comes someone!" said Peter, starting up anxiously. "I hear them in the passage."

Martin nodded. "Fru Roland said she'd be sending in a midmorning snack. You were sleeping so hard, we didn't wake you for breakfast."

It was Gunnuf who opened the little door, but as he stepped through, Martin and Peter each gave a shout of surprise and welcome, for close behind him, with a plate of coffeecakes in her hand, came Inga Holm.

Her eyes were serious, and even anxious, and though she managed a swift smile in greeting, her face quickly became grave again. "Make a good meal now, Martin," she said, deftly arranging a little table, "because you and I have a dangerous trip ahead of us."

"Inga!" cried Martin. "You know something about Mother and Petra."

"Yes, I do, Martin," she replied, with a directness which he appreciated. "They were on their way to us, but the lame man and Kurt are looking for them, and they hid in a cave where Petra and I have taken refuge before now. I went there this morning for shelter from the rain, as I often do, and found them. Martin, you are in grave danger, and so are they. You are to be held as hostages, if they can lay hands on you, to bring pressure on your father. Our place is a good place for you to hide, all together, until you can get out of the country."

"Hostages!" exclaimed Martin. "We just can't be caught, Inga! Think what it would mean! But we'd put you in too great danger if we went to the saeter."

"O Martin! We're all working together. Everything's dangerous, but this is at least a chance. We have a little secret storage closet. Let's get going, as fast as we can."

Martin thought a moment. "You're right, Inga," he agreed, and fell straight to planning. "Kurt and Hartsell are on the mountain now?"

"Yes, but they have gone far above the cave. If we hurry, I think we can get to the folks. I know many places to hide on that mountain. But, Martin, if only we had some way to get word to someone in Valcos who could help get you out!"

"Ole!" said Martin swiftly. "He's the one to help us. We'll take his homing pigeons with us. This is certainly the emergency. Come, Inga. Good-by, Peter! Keep a stiff upper lip. It may be that you will be the first one over the new route after all. I've thought of a way now, and we'll work it out, but Petra and Mother and I can't wait for that, I'm afraid. We'll have to get out fast. See you in England!" There was a quick, firm handshake, and Martin and Inga were gone.

Inga had already told the Rolands her story, and now they stood ready to speed Martin on his way.

"Herr Roland," said Martin, speaking swiftly, "I want to say, before I go, I think I've got a way worked out—a new route that will be pretty safe, for a while at least. I still have to work out details, though. How will I get them to you?"

"I'll see to that," said Inga, and all of them knew that promise would be kept.

"It was the valley that was troubling me," Martin hurried on, "but a false-bottomed boat could go down that river. That would work for a while, at least, and then we'll think up something new. Perhaps, too, a hay wagon with a special compartment could be used. Ole would help with the boat, I know that."

"And our folks have a farm down that way. They'd help," said Inga.

"We'll keep on working, and we won't be out of touch with you," said Herr Roland. "We'll get word back and forth with the help of Inga and some of our other young Norwegians. And one of these days you'll be back, Martin."

"I will that!" said Martin fervently. "I have a feeling that the sooner I am gone now, the sooner I'll be able to help get things straight."

"Go then, and God be with you," said the old professor, his voice somewhat husky, but steady nevertheless. "You did your job here, Martin, and did it well. Now it's time for you to go on to the next one."

"That's right," agreed Fru Roland briskly. "I don't see why anyone should look so sad about it." She blew her nose energetically and gave Martin a hearty hug. "You've been wanting to get into that training like Sigurd. Go, and do a good job. But, O Martin," she added, her voice breaking in spite of her efforts, "be careful, won't you? They're not fooling, you know."

"I know," said Martin gently. "But Inga knows these mountains inside out. We'll be careful."

It was hard to keep from breaking down himself, and he was thankful when Fru Roland said, giving herself an impatient shake, "Oh, my goodness, we aren't going to be geese enough to forget those pigeons, I hope," and ran to get the basket.

That made the parting a little easier, and they were all smiling as he and Inga set off up the trail. When would he set foot on this familiar path again? He didn't dare to think of that now. He must think, rather, of what lay ahead.

Martin and Inga walked swiftly along, thankful for their familiarity with the mountain. "The lame man and Kurt, may, of course, be on their way down," Inga warned. "If ever we've needed to be cautious, Martin, this is the time. So much is at stake now."

Martin nodded, his eyes as serious as hers. They climbed onward in silence, listening keenly for any unfamiliar sound. Used as they were to the trails, they made good progress, and had almost reached the point where they should leave the main trail to reach the cave, when Martin paused suddenly to listen, seized Inga's hand, and drew her swiftly to shelter behind some large rocks, his face tense and alert.

Inga had heard the sound too, and her eyes were big with alarm as she looked at Martin, for now they heard again that halting step that had given them so much trouble. A few moments later, Kurt and Hartsell came around the bend.

"But I tell you I know they're here, somewhere on this mountain, and not far away," Hartsell was saying angrily. "I saw them start off, and if I'd followed alone and not waited for you it would have been better. You don't seem to want to find them. You're no true German. I believe you want them to get away."

"I've been trying my best to find them, and you know it. I've been looking in old caves—finding all our remembered hiding places. But if they do get away, what of it?" Kurt answered, stung to recklessness. "They've always been kind to me. Why should I want to torment them? I hate myself for what I'm doing."

"Weakling!" sneered Hartsell. "You'd better make up your mind to succeed in this day's work, or you can picture for yourself what will happen to you, especially if I should take it into my head to repeat that speech."

"Well, then, let's go around the mountain. There's one more place I know, but I warn you it's hard climbing. We branch off and climb upward again."

Inga looked at Martin with sick fear in her face. Martin leaned forward, his eyes angry, his face tense. Well, then, they knew about the cave where Mother and Petra were hiding—Kurt knew about it, after all. But they needn't think they were going to get there first, to find his mother and sister trapped. He could outrun them, and he would. He would have the head start too. He would dash up the mountainside and be there before they were, to warn Mother and Petra. They would all at least make a rush for safety together. Martin poised himself for a swift spurt of running.

XVIII

The "Viking" Sets Sail

M ARTIN WAS ABOUT TO SPRING from his hiding place and make a dash up the mountain when Inga clutched his arm. "Wait!" her lips formed the word soundlessly. For Kurt had passed the obscure little path that led to the cave where Fru Engeland and Petra were. He was leading the way past them down the trail, and now he took a path that branched sharply upward.

"Oh, that's the way he meant!" breathed Inga, when the two were out of sight. "They're going back up the mountain toward the saeter. That trail leads to some of our cowpaths and pastures. But, Martin, they're going to find some hard going. The boys always work on that trail in the summer, and of course there's been no chance for that this year."

"Will this give us time to rescue the folks and get them to your cabin?" asked Martin swiftly.

"I hope so. But we've got to work fast. And we've got to keep hidden from the main trail as we go. There's not much of a path, either, but we'll get there. We'll have to hurry."

In the little cave up the mountainside, Fru Engeland and Petra were waiting anxiously. Many times
that morning Petra had ventured to the entrance and
peered out, and now, at last, she gave a low exclamation, "Mother! They're almost here! Martin and
Inga!" She flew down the rough little path, her mother
following. "Why didn't you give the old signal?" she
greeted them. "We would have met you on the little
saeter path and saved some time."

"Not safe to give any kind of signal," explained
Martin in a low tone. "Hartsell and Kurt are still on
the mountain, and we don't know where."

"Then do we dare set out?" asked Fru Engeland.

"We have to," said Martin. "Kurt may know this
cave, after all. We have to get to a safer place."

"They're going up the trail on the other side," explained Inga swiftly. "We must try to get to the cabin
before they catch sight of us."

Crouching down, keeping close to the rocks and
trees, the little group filed silently up the rough path,
Inga leading, Petra close behind, Martin keeping
watch in the rear.

"The part I'm most afraid of," whispered Inga, "is
the little hayfield between the woods and the saeter.
We'll be in plain sight there. The hay has been cut."

At the edge of the wood they paused to reconnoiter. The saeter cabin lay only a few rods away. There
they would find comparative safety. But the open hayfield stretched between, with its rows of low fences
over which the hay was spread, Norwegian fashion,
to dry.

"We'll have to make a run for it," said Martin. "Cross it just as fast as we can. Come, Mother." His heart was beating fast, and he felt his mother's hand icy-cold as he grasped it to help her in the rush across the stubble.

They were halfway across. Surely they would make it. But now Inga gave a terrified whisper: "Look! Over there on the trail! Kurt and the lame man!"

Suddenly, in their desperate need, Martin remembered something. It flashed into his mind that, years ago, they used to use those hay-draped fences for play tents. Now they were to be put to a grimmer use. "Quick!" he ordered, his voice low and tense. "Duck under those hay fences!"

They crouched together in the long, dim tent, the protecting hay on each side of them. "If only they didn't see us first," whispered Petra, her face white and strained as she watched intently the men on the other side of the saeter.

Suddenly Inga drew in her breath sharply. "They are going across the footbridge," she said in a strangled whisper. "We never use that till it's been taken care of in the spring. It won't hold! It won't hold!"

In terrified silence, the four under the hay fences watched as Kurt and Hartsell hesitated on the little bridge. Their voices, raised in argument, came clearly through the mountain air.

"You fooled me once before when you said those caves would be safe for the guns," Hartsell accused angrily. "How can you expect me to trust your judgment about this bridge? It looks all right to me, and it's our only chance to cut them off. I'm sure they're there. I doubt if you want to find them."

"I don't care if you trust my judgment or not, and I don't much care what happens to myself or to you either," retorted Kurt, "but that bridge isn't safe."

"Afraid, eh?" taunted Hartsell. "A lame man can take it, but you can't. You come with me. Those are orders. Understand?" He started defiantly across the narrow old footbridge. "Come on, you!" he shouted, and Kurt, hesitating for a moment, followed. "See! It's safe! I told you! We're almost over!"

And then suddenly a cry went up as the four watched, for the bridge gave way and plunged down into the rocky chasm far below. There was a moment of stunned silence following the crash. At last Martin broke it with the grave words, "They will do no more harm to Norway—those two."

In spite of an inevitable feeling of relief, no one felt like talking, and it was a solemn and quiet little group that crept out from hiding and crossed the field to the saeter cabin.

Margot threw the door wide in welcome. "What has happened? How white you are!" she exclaimed.

She and Karen listened in shocked amazement to their story, and when it was told, Karen said soberly, "They came once too often, uninvited, and bringing danger."

Margot nodded silently. Then she sprang up. "This has been a terrible ordeal for you all. I will get something for you to eat," she said in her practical way. "You surely look as though you need some refreshment, and some rest."

"But first," said Martin, "we must get that message off to Ole. We will send both pigeons, to make sure. We must take no chances. He has his good ship, the *Viking*, hidden for just such a time as this. He and I have talked of it—talked and planned. We will hide here today and get away tonight. If only there were some safe, quick way to get down the mountain!"

"I know!" Petra gave a sudden, excited cry. "Isn't it about the time you send bales of hay down the mountainside with a rope and pulley and wires? I used to love to watch that and wish I could go down the mountain that way. Couldn't we be well wrapped in hay and let down over the cliff to your farm in the valley?"

"Good thought, Petra!" cried her brother.

"Oh, yes, and how good it is that everything is ready!" exclaimed Margot. "Father and Uncle were up last week and examined it all and put it in good order, for it is nearly time to send the hay down."

"That takes care of that!" said Martin. "Ole has the *Viking* hidden not so far from there, and he has arranged a secret compartment in it, for an emergency. He's been getting ready for just such a time as this. He's made a point of going out at night, and fairly long distances, for extra good fishing, and they've let him do pretty much as he pleases, he's such a valuable man to them."

"Yes, he would be the one—perhaps the only one who could have a good chance of getting us down the fjord without trouble," said Fru Engeland.

"You're not afraid to travel in a bale of hay, Mother?" asked Martin.

For the first time that day, they all smiled. "I'll love it," she replied. "Let's get the message off to him without delay—to stand by ready for us tonight."

It was a restless, uneasy day, for they all knew that new searching parties might be sent out. The Engelands stayed close indoors, ready to take refuge, at a moment's notice, in the little secret closet. Margot and Karen and Inga, though they seemed very busy with their usual chores, kept a careful watch for intruders.

The afternoon dragged by, and it seemed evening would never come, but when the time came at last to set off on the night's strange travel, the farewells were hard indeed to say. All of them were thankful that there was so much to do, so many odd preparations to make in connection with their unusual method of departure.

Martin longed to be the first over the cliff, but he felt he must stay to help with the pulley on the first trips, so Petra, well wrapped in hay, was the first to be lowered over the edge.

Her heart was beating fast, and all of them looked anxious, for this was an entirely new experience. But it was a thrilling one, and, well-protected as she was by the hay, she felt a wild exhilaration as she went swiftly down the mountain. It was like flying, and she was almost sorry to find herself safe on the ground so soon. Fru Engeland came next, and then Margot and Inga together sent Martin speeding on his way.

"We'll get out of these hay packages, and then you wait here!" whispered Martin. "I think I know where Ole is."

It seemed a long time that they waited, resting on their beds of hay, but at last Martin returned and said softly: "Ole's waiting for us! Come now!"

They were thankful that there was no moon, but even so the Norwegian summer night was not very dark. Ole had painted his white *Viking* gray, for better protection, but its slim, graceful lines made it still the most beautiful ship on the fjord, as well as the fastest.

He helped them aboard in silence, and placed them where they could readily take refuge in the small, secret compartment he had arranged. But no one wanted to go in unless it was necessary, and as the *Viking* set sail for the last journey they were to have down the fjord for many a day, they stood in the dim twilight, their hearts full as they watched the familiar scenes slip by.

It was an anxious trip, but since Ole had made it a point to set out at night for more than one fishing trip, nobody challenged him now, and they sailed safely down the fjord.

"Go in, now, for a little," he said softly, as they neared the mouth of the fjord, "until we pass this spot. I'll knock when you can come out. We may be challenged here."

From their cramped shelter, they heard the patrols questioning Ole, heard his matter-of-fact, easy replies. "Oh, *ja*, sure, I often fish down here. There's a good run, I hear, farther down the coast. I think I can pick up a little crew and have a good catch. We need more fish to pack."

Now they were on their way again, threading between the islands down the coast. Ole gave a knock and they came out once more, chuckling over Ole's "little crew and good catch," watching in the soft, pearly light, the rocky island *skerries* that edged the coast, the steep farms that stretched up the mountainside.

Through the quiet night they talked, making plans for sending messages, making plans for future escape trips out of Norway. Martin outlined his route of escape to Sweden, and Ole approved it. "I can help," he said. "They don't suspect the old sailor yet, and I think I can see to it that they won't. I am glad you told me of Hans. In this emergency I should know. Together we will work—Hans and Peter and Eric, Jorgenson, the Rolands, the Holms—many more of us. And you in England will do your part. We will get the men through, and the messages."

"Yes," agreed Martin. "Between us we will give the Nazis as much trouble as possible, and Norway as much help."

"Here I must leave you for a while," said Ole, toward morning. "We are pretty safe to put in at this island for a short time. I must arrange for that little fishing crew I need on my return journey. We must see to it that we have a good catch to show when we get home—though it won't be half so interesting as the one we had that we didn't show when we left home," he added laughing. "Besides, I have a message to send, and the homing pigeons cannot take it. I have them here, though, for you to take with you. They too are ready to work for Norway in case we should need them."

He was smiling as he spoke, but he was smiling even more when he returned. "We go on together, the

Viking and you folks and I, to the islands, and then—"
He broke off abruptly and would say no more, but his
smile was broad, and they understood it as late the
next day they neared the islands.

For a ship was waiting there that they knew well,
and on the deck stood a captain they had been longing to see. And now a boat was lowered, and there
was bustle and activity as the new passengers came
aboard. There were smiles, but there were tears too,
for their joy was great, and it had seemed this time
would never come.

"I want to hug all of you at once!" exclaimed Captain Engeland.

But the lumps in their throats melted away, and
all of them laughed as Ole cried out, "Not me!"

They talked fast, for there was much to tell and
many plans to make. "These folks of yours, Captain Engeland, you have a good right to be proud
of them," said Ole. "Little by little they will tell you
everything, and you will be surprised at what they
have accomplished—encouraged too, for it proves
what these young folks of ours can do for Norway."

"I know that well," Captain Engeland replied, and
his eyes were shining as he smiled down at his wife.
He put his hand on Martin's shoulder and gave Petra
a hug. "I have already heard more than one report that
has made me proud."

"Ole wasn't so bad, either, Father," said Martin,
smiling at his old friend. "And he still has them fooled."

"O Ole, I wish you were going with us!" cried
Petra, a lump in her throat.

"Yes, Ole," said Captain Engeland. "I have arranged for Martin's training in the same work as Sigurd's. You should be with that outfit." He was smiling now. "You would make the boys work hard and fast to keep up with you, from what I hear."

"I'd do that," chuckled Ole. "Maybe I'll come over yet!"

"And Petra and I?" asked Fru Engeland eagerly. "What do we do?"

"There's work in plenty for you—Norwegian women and girls already are busy in England, and you two will find your work."

Ole's blue eyes were bright as he looked from one to the other. "There's a lot left to do in Norway," he said. "You did your part there, Martin, you and Petra. Your mother too. Now you'll be working in England, each in your own way, and it will be a good way. I know that well. But don't forget to come back to Norway."

The engines of the big boat were vibrating, the men taking their stations, ready to go. Ole went over the side and stood on his deck, looking up at them. They knew well the little ceremony with which a Norwegian ship should begin its journey, and now all of them together, the captain and his family and the crew on the big boat, Ole alone on the deck of the little *Viking*, stood at attention, serious eyes on Norway's flag.

And over the quiet waters, above the vibration of the engines, the lapping of the waves against the boats, came the words of Norway's national anthem, as they sang it, all together.

"Yes, we love with fond devotion
Norway's mountain domes,
Rising storm-lashed o'er the ocean,
With their thousand homes."

"Long ago, when you were little, you learned to sing those stirring words," said Captain Engeland. "Now you have proved you know what they mean."

They were getting under way now, and the little *Viking* was setting its course for home. Martin and Petra stood at the rail waving to Ole, watching until the little ship had disappeared from sight among the islands.

As they drew near the end of their journey, they were at the rail again, watching the shores of England come into clearer and clearer view. " 'Norway's mountain domes, rising storm-lashed o'er the ocean, with their thousand homes,' " Petra murmured, and turned to her brother. "That describes our Norway. England looks lots different, doesn't it, Martin?" she said, and her voice trembled a little.

"Yes, it does. But, Petra, don't forget that someday we're going back."

Petra nodded, and stood silently watching the shore line, clearly defined now.

"Look, Martin! What a big pier! And, why, there are Sigurd and Ruggles!" she cried joyfully. "They've got leave! They've come to meet us!"

"Yes, they must have been waiting and watching like good ones to be here!" exclaimed Martin. "See, they are greeting us with the Victory salute!"

Hardly was the gangplank down before the two boys rushed on deck. "You're here! You're here!"

shouted Sigurd. "Oh, we have so much to show you! Lots of Norwegians waiting to greet you! We've got a little feast, with *gjetöst* we brought from the saeter!"

"You're going to find friends here, and plenty of work," said Ruggles, shaking hands heartily all around. "I suppose, like the rest of your countrymen, your hearts will be in Norway. But I can say, from the bottom of mine, "Welcome to England, and to work with us for victory!"